A Lady in Doubt

A Lady in Doubt

Annabel Wynne

St. Martin's Press
New York

Library of Congress Cataloging in Publication Data

Wynne, Annabel.
  Lady in doubt.

  I. Title.
PZ4.W9887Lad 1979 [PR6073.Y7] 823′.9′14 78-19395
ISBN 0-312-46424-X

A Lady in Doubt

CHAPTER ONE

'Lady Lacey's compliments, Miss, and she considers the pearl drop earrings would complete Miss Brown's toilette nicely, if you would be so kind as to spare 'em for this evening, Miss.'

Alice gave a small sigh of exasperation as her eyes met those of her maid in the mirror. The maid's eyes held frank disapproval. 'I could say I'd mislaid 'em, Miss— the pearl earrings—or sent 'em to be repaired. Only give me the word. Lady Lacey's got no right to make free of your jewelry, and it's my belief you ought to tell her so. Beg pardon, Miss, I'm sure.'

Alice silenced her maid with a reproving look and turned to the corner of the large bedroom where a dark woman was locking up a press with trembling old hands. 'Bring me my jewel-case, please, Betty-Lou,' she said.

The old woman mumbled unintelligibly to herself and obstinately turned the key of the press.

'Betty-Lou!' said Alice sharply. 'My jewels, if you please.'

'Enough, enough,' shrilled the old woman, turning and glaring defiantly.

Alice sighed again. What with a grasping sister-in-law on one side, who made as free of Alice's possessions as if she had a legal right to them, and her mother's temperamental old coloured maid on the other, life became extremely irritating at times even for a great heiress, a beauty, and the biggest catch of the London season.

'You give that key to me and stop muttering evil like you was a witch,' her little maid said vigorously, trying to force open the old woman's hand. 'You got no business to be so contrary with Miss's jewels when she's so good to you.'

5

'Now, Mary . . .' chided Alice. Betty-Lou had been her mother's faithful servant—first slave, then maid—for over thirty years and Alice felt duty-bound to tolerate her senile delusions.

Betty-Lou grumbled fiercely under her breath as she unlocked the press, returned the key to some inner part of her clothing, drew out the jewel-case of old frayed Spanish leather, and prepared for another trembling search for its little key.

'Give over, do, and let me manage it,' cried Mary in healthy young exasperation for all the delay.

'Mine,' said the old dark woman, and angrily clutched the case in her bosom. 'Mine. All, all mine. Never you touch it. Go away.' Eventually, with the greatest tact, she was persuaded to bring the case to the dressing-table and open it.

Alice lifted her pearl-drop earrings from their little velvet tray. They were Caribbean pearls of no great value, but had often been worn by her mother, and in memory of her mother Alice herself wore them frequently. Lending them out to Clara Brown would be some sort of desecration.

She chose a pair of diamond roses with pearl hearts. Betty-Lou made a grab for them. 'No!' she quavered. 'Mine!' But Alice dexterously slipped them past the old dark trembling fingers and gave them to Mary. 'Take these to Lady Lacey with my compliments,' she said.

Something had to be done. Betty-Lou must be persuaded to give up this last tiny household task and retire away from London to Holt Lacey. She was too infirm to be given a cottage on the estate, but she could live out her last years by a warm fire in the manor house kitchen and cease to inflict her avid possessiveness on Alice.

And Laura Lacey would have to be told that she must give up these ever-growing encroachments on Alice's things or—find another house to live in.

6

Alice stared at herself in the mirror. Big, worried, dark eyes gazed back at her from a long, oval face with clear olive skin. To her own mind, the mouth was too wide for the present-day rosebud fashion, but she did not realize how irresistibly its generous smile lit up her classic features. Oh dear! No doubt there was going to be an unpleasant scene over the jewels, and no doubt Geoffrey would join his wife against his sister, but Alice would win. She would have to, because life was rapidly becoming impossible. Tomorrow she would tackle the problem squarely, but meanwhile a ball awaited.

'Mary, that side piece of hair is slipping,' Alice told her maid when she returned. 'Can't you fasten it more securely? It will need another pin at the back.'

'Lady Lacey said the earrings were too handsome for a young girl,' Mary reported. 'She is wearing them herself and lending Miss Clara her pearl studs.'

Alice flushed with anger, but let it pass in another deep sigh. Heavens and earth! She must not permit so small a thing to sour her evening. Yet, really! Laura would be demanding to wear the Lacey emeralds next.

How Alice wished her father had not died! How she loathed living under the nominal care of her brother and her brother's wife Laura, and being forced into unwilling friendship with Laura's sister, Clara Brown.

She wished sometimes that her father had not favoured her so conspicuously in his will. It gave Laura what she considered fair grounds for grievance, although lately her demands had been going much too far. Alice felt that her brother ought to check them, but he had become noticeably lax in this way over the past few months. Ought Alice to ask them to leave her London house and take the petulant young Clara with them? But it was so convenient to have them with her during the London season. After all, no young lady in mid-Victorian England could live in her own house and go to social functions without a constant chaperone. Alice had welcomed their arrival and turned a blind eye to the fact that Clara's millinery bills found their way into her own with regular persistence. She liked to be helpful, but it was all getting out of hand.

'Are you ready, Alice?' A voice came from the doorway, and Clara appeared, a plump, fretful creature in a gown that was too tightly laced at the waist. Her eyes were clear light blue of a good colour and her ash-blonde hair soft and abundant. Nature had been kind to Clara Brown, but she spoilt the natural effect with a peevish expression and the liberal use of hot curling tongs.

'Yes.' Alice rose to her feet. 'Mary, where is my reticule?'

'Here, Miss, and I have your shawl over my arm.' Mary placed a bonnet of the very smallest dimensions on her mistress's head and stood back for Alice to pass through the door. Clara retreated across the wide landing—she had to. The skirts of the two girls touched, but their shoulders were over a yard apart. From tiny waists their dresses billowed out wider and wider to the floor, and standing side by side, they took up more room than a four-poster bed.

'It is time to go. We shall be late,' said Lady Lacey as she came down from her bedchamber on the upper floor. 'Well!' she added. 'How charming you both look tonight!'

Alice, the taller of the two and the one with the greater poise, was wearing a dress of pale green silk gauze with two deep flounces at the hem. Her skirts swung free of her feet over one of the new cage crinolines made from the finest watch-spring steel in Mr Thompson's workshops. Because a cold May was leading into a chilly June and because she liked the effect, Alice had chosen to wear a lightly padded petticoat between her crinoline and her dress. The silk lay softly over it like a huge flowery bell, light and free.

Clara had been forced to be contented with one of Laura's discarded horsehair crinolines, helped out with

8

three starched petticoats. Even that had not given her the width she felt necessary, so she had added yet another petticoat of red flannel in a final desperate effort to achieve airy amplitude. But the gain in weight offset the gain in circumference, and her jealous eyes told her that she looked lumpy beside Alice's effortless elegance. And her pale blue mousseline dress should have been—she felt—a few shades brighter. The widowed Queen Victoria might still be wearing black for her dear, dead Consort, but London had cast off its last shreds of mourning and was frankly gay this year.

'Come, then,' Laura Lacey said. 'The carriage is waiting.' She was fair-haired and blue-eyed like her young sister, but her skin had lost its early bloom and her hair had never been so abundant as Clara's. For party wear a huge chignon of false hair was pinned to the back of her head, and over this her maid had cunningly arranged Laura's own thin tresses. A small wreath of artificial flowers aided the deception well enough. Now that Laura's husband-hunting days were over, all her attention was devoted to her clothes. She was wearing mauve silk with gold fringes over a crinoline of wide steel bands let into a cambric petticoat. She walked down the centre of the landing, keeping clear of walls, for she knew that those bands were not of such fine quality as Alice's and would soon lose their shape. For the same reason, she glided to the top of the staircase with tiny, rapid steps. Confusion lay in wait for ladies who caught their feet in their bottom hoop.

'I am glad that Lady Arthur's house has decently wide stairs,' Clara said. 'I lost half the roses off my pink satin on those poky bannisters at the Clark's last week.'

The staircase they now descended was beyond criticism—wide and curving and shallow-stepped to accommodate each of them generously. Bitter resentment rose unchecked to Lady Lacey's mind. This house—so utterly satisfactory in every way—should have belonged to her husband and herself, not Alice! Why had Sir Walter

9

Lacey, wicked old reprobate, chosen to leave so very much to his daughter? His duty was to pass on everything intact to his son, child of his first wife and Alice's half-brother. That was how English fortunes were amassed and maintained. Alice should have received a few thousand pounds, and the London house and both the country estates should have gone to Sir Geoffrey. 'For Alice had the West Indian plantation from her mother,' Lady Lacey assured herself for the thousandth irritated time, 'and she could always have commanded a home with me and Geoffrey. No woman is fit to be in charge of such large property—Lacey property,' fumed her ladyship, her mind following a well-worn groove. 'And then she will marry and the Lacey lands go out of the family for ever. And dear Alice is so strong-minded! How are we to stop her choosing some wicked fortune hunter?'

'I cannot understand why my husband does not join us tonight,' Laura said aloud as she buttoned her gloves. 'He cannot be at the House as it is Wednesday.'

'Poor Geoffrey has to spend so much time on my West Indian affairs,' said Alice pacifically. 'He has been busy about them these last three months. So much trouble and so little reward! I have begged him to let the matter slide but he is too kind.' There! Surely that would sweeten Laura's face a little? It was a handsome apology for something for which Alice felt no need to be grateful. She liked to handle her own affairs, but in this one case Geoffrey had had to act for her, and she wished he had not made such a bother of it, continually grumbling whilst telling Alice that the whole question was beyond a lady's comprehension.

'Indeed, you would be lost without your brother to guide you,' remarked Laura, brightening at the thought.

The front door opened abruptly and Sir Geoffrey Lacey hurried in, a big, florid, red-faced man with a complexion more suited to a country squire than a politician.

10

'Ah! You have decided to come with us after all,' cried Laura, greatly gratified. 'We can wait while you change. I am sure Alice will not mind.'

Geoffrey's eyes swept round to his half-sister. He seemed to be in the grip of some strong emotion.

'Is anything wrong?' asked Alice, for he was staring at her with an expression which she found hard to understand. 'What is the matter, Geoffrey? We are going to the Arthur's ball. Laura told you about it at breakfast this morning. Surely you cannot disapprove?'

His eyes swung slowly down from that ridiculously small bonnet to the white cashmere shawl now swathing her shoulders, the ruby pendant at her throat, the wide shimmering yardage of her dress, the small green gloves bound with white kid and the narrow green satin slippers barely visible beneath.

'You are not going to any ball, Alice,' he said harshly. 'Go up to your room and take all that flummery off. When I think what that dress must have cost, I shudder.'

'Geoffrey!' cried Alice in indignation.

Laura quickly intervened. A row between her husband and his wealthy half-sister would be disastrous at the moment, with Geoffrey's necessary attendance at Parliament, Clara's coming out and no London house of their own to work from. 'Please do not take a dislike to Alice's gown, my dear,' she said ingratiatingly. 'It may be a little low on the bosom, but that is the height of fashion now, I assure you. And Alice has been so kind in lending me these diamond earrings ...'

'They were not hers to lend,' said Geoffrey. 'Nor are those jewels round her neck. Take them off, Alice. We have been most bitterly deceived.'

Geoffrey Lacey was not normally a rude man, and his manners towards his half-sister were usually polite, if stiff. Like his wife, he resented the fact that their father had left the Lacey property to Alice whilst he had only received the Derbyshire lands that had come with his own mother. But none of the property had been entailed, and the old man had had the right to do as he wished with it. 'There will be no ball tonight,' Sir Geoffrey said grimly.

'But my dear!' exclaimed his wife. 'How can you be so cruel? Percy has promised to be in close attendance and to find partners for Clara when he is not squiring Alice...'

'Percy may as well take his attentions elsewhere,' Sir Geoffrey said, striding past the ladies into the dining-room. 'As will all the rest.' He laughed and kicked at the dying fire in the grate. 'Alice should not be going to balls at all. She should be sitting at home and helping with the mending. We have all been grossly taken in. Alice is a pauper.'

Laura closed the door against the interested gaze of the butler and footman and the frightened eyes of Alice's little maid.

Alice herself moved in a dream. She did not like her brother much, but she knew him to be a careful, calculating man. His present behaviour was right out of character, but he would not act like this without good cause.

Alice Lacey a *pauper*? She felt quite numb. What did it mean?

Sir Geoffrey turned to face the three ladies. Laura ran up to him and grasped his arm. 'Are you well, my love?' she enquired with fashionable concern. 'You have been overworking shockingly. They should not ask you to spend so many hours in Parliament.'

Geoffrey put her hand aside. 'I have not been at the House of Commons,' he said. 'I have been with our attorney.' And he paused. The blow he was about to deliver was a hard one, and Sir Geoffrey was not by nature a cruel man.

They all waited. Attorneys dealt with gentlemen's affairs, and none of the three ladies had the faintest idea what could have kept Sir Geoffrey so long in a solicitor's office.

'Well?' prompted Laura at last.

'We have been interrogating a young man lately returned from the West Indies,' said the baronet heavily.

'I wish that my affairs there were not in such a muddle,' Alice said, 'but if the whole of my plantation is lost, it is no great matter.'

'This is a very great matter,' Sir Geoffrey said ominously.

'Please tell us, my dear,' said Laura, 'and if there are any little legal difficulties between you and Alice, I am sure they can be sorted out without unpleasantness.'

'This all started,' Sir Geoffrey informed them, 'at the end of last year, when we, Mr Sellop and myself, received some startling news which required checking in the West Indies.'

'What startling news? Was it about me? Why was I not informed?' interrupted Alice immediately.

Her half-brother turned his broad red face to hers. 'What do you know of your mother's coming to England?' he asked in return.

'Why, very little,' Alice said in surprise.

'She lived alone, did she not, on her plantation after she was left an orphan?'

'I believe so. But it was only for a few months. Then my father—our father—came out from England and married her and brought her back to his home.'

'So we all understood,' said Geoffrey Lacey heavily.

'Is it not true?' cried Alice in bewilderment.

'In every particular but one. My father did not marry your mother. He brought her home to Holt Lacey and introduced her to everybody as his wife, but no trace of the marriage exists. No marriage ever took place. Your mother died Amelie Lestrange as she was born. She never became Lady Lacey at all.'

Alice sank into a chair. Laura and Clara had cried out in conventional horror, but Alice made no sound. She was thinking back to her childhood and the beloved, beautiful, gentle figure that had guided it. She recalled

13

the long oval face, so like her own, framed in dark ringlets as the fashion then was, the dark eyes and the sweet, wide smile—her mother, performing words of charity—her mother, bending over a prayer-book—the shining gold cross that always lay on her mother's bosom . . .

'I don't believe it,' said Alice flatly.

Opposition always brought out the worst in Geoffrey. 'Your belief has very little to do with the case,' he said brusquely. 'Mr Sellop put out a most careful search, and he is entirely satisfied that no marriage took place in the West Indies.'

'Then they were married in England,' cried Alice, springing up. 'And you have behaved most wrongly, Geoffrey, in listening to these disgraceful calumnies! How could you? Was not my mother a most loving mama to you? She treated you in every way as if you were her own—you must admit it. Geoffrey,' she crossed over and laid her hand on his arm. 'You loved her almost as much as I did. How can you let them say such dreadful things about your own step-mama?'

'I do not wish to do the lady's memory harm,' said her half-brother gruffly. 'She was always very good to me.'

'And I am delighted to hear you say so!' cried Alice warmly. 'Please never raise the subject again, Geoffrey, or it would be impossible for you to remain in my house. I must see Mr Sellop and try to have such a dreadful slander . . .' Her voice died down. Something in her brother's face stopped her.

'This is *not* your house. You have no house. No lands, no rents, no funds, nothing.'

'What do you mean?' asked Alice, and she started to tremble. Was it her imagination, or had Laura and Clara drawn away from her? They were certainly staring at her in a very strange way. But then it was all so strange. Alice put her hand to her head.

'My father,' went on Sir Geoffrey, 'left all the Lacey property to *Alice Lacey*.'

'And he had no right to do it,' cried Laura viciously, speaking her mind for the very first time.

'Alice Lacey does not exist,' said Geoffrey. 'You, Alice, are Alice Lestrange. You take your mother's name, if indeed you are entitled to a name at all.'

'But father meant me to have it all,' cried Alice. 'He said so expressly in his will. And he commanded you to observe his wishes with the greatest care, Geoffrey,' she remembered.

'Nevertheless, it is impossible for you to inherit,' said her half-brother. 'There is no person *Alice Lacey* such as he named. Therefore that part of the will is invalid. Everything reverts to the natural heir. To me.'

Alice felt as if there were some impediment to her breathing. She sank back into the chair, trembling so hard that the ruby drops in her ears were set a-quiver.

'And the London property. This house?' asked Laura eagerly.

'It all belongs to me, my dear,' said Geoffrey, and he set back his head and widened his shoulders. He had not been a poor man before, for the Derbyshire property that had come with his mother was rich in coal and Sir Walter had shown what amounted to genius in developing it. Profits from Derbyshire coal had financed the building of railways along the northern borders of the Lacey lands in the West Country. Booming railways had demanded yet more coal and each enterprise had enhanced the other. No, Sir Geoffrey had not been a poor man. But now he was very wealthy indeed and there need be no bounds to his parliamentary ambitions. Today he held a small post in the Admiralty. Within a very short time he could hope to be an under-secretary. In a year or so, if his party stayed in power, he would get a higher promotion, and thereafter the path ran straight upwards towards a peerage and a seat in the House of Lords.

'*Poor* Alice,' said Clara Brown in a small uncertain voice.

15

It was the only note of sympathy expressed that evening, and it cut through the cloud of shock and bewilderment that surrounded Alice. She raised her head. But Clara's remark had been a trivial reaction. Her glance of pity had already been replaced by a glittering calculation of what this change in Laura's fortunes would mean to herself.

'Alice has had enough good things to last her for the rest of her life,' said Laura callously. 'She was always her father's favourite and now she must pay the penalty. The Lord giveth, and,' concluded Lady Lacey with satisfaction, 'the Lord taketh away.'

'Laura, do you realize all this pretty furniture is yours now?' asked Clara, much struck.

'Pretty it may be, but smart it certainly is not,' said Laura, eyeing the dining-room chairs with distaste. 'I will have the upholsterers in to replace those seats before a week is out. I could never understand why Alice put up with that old-fashioned brocade for so long!'

'I must not break down,' Alice was telling herself. 'I must keep control.' She tried to steady her shaking fingers. 'Geoffrey,' she said, 'you cannot expect me to take all this—this—disastrous news on your word alone. I must consult Mr Sellop. I have that right.'

'You have no rights at all, Alice, and you must learn to get used to it,' he replied roundly.

'Then please, as a favour to me,' she said, 'let me hear from some legal source exactly where I stand.'

'I have told you where you stand, Alice. Nothing of my father's comes to you.'

'What of my mother's plantation in the West Indies?' Small and unprofitable as that was, it would still give Alice some tiny right to hold her head up in the world.

'It appears that you have no claim on that either.'

'I do not understand. You do admit at least that I am my mother's child. If she had property, does it not belong to me now that she is dead?'

'Of course your mother had no property of her own

16

when she died,' said Lady Lacey, turning on her. 'It all became Sir Walter's when she married him.'

Sir Geoffrey favoured his wife with a quelling look. 'Sir Walter did *not* marry Alice's mother, my love,' he said. 'That is the whole point.'

Laura flushed angrily. 'Well I'm sure the law would say she gave up her rights to everything when she—when—as soon as she behaved so outrageously,' she huffed. 'And Clara, go to your room at once. It is most unfitting for a young girl to listen while matters such as these are being discussed.'

Clara tossed her head and made a move towards the door but did not actually leave the room.

'Then I can go to the West Indies and take possession of Frenchman's Point Plantation?' Alice persisted.

'I think not,' Sir Geoffrey shuffled his feet on the hearthrug uncomfortably. 'We will talk about it another time, if you please Alice.'

'I would rather know now,' she replied. 'If I am not the owner of Frenchman's Point, then who is?'

'Probably Betty-Lou,' said her brother.

'*Betty-Lou?*'

'Yes. I would rather not have brought this subject up in family conversation, Alice, but since you force me— do you know who Betty-Lou's parents were?'

'Her mother was one of my grandfather's slaves at Frenchman's Point.'

'And her father?'

'A—a—a white man of some sort, I presume. My mother told me that she was of mixed parentage.'

'She did not tell you that Betty-Lou's father was your own grandfather?'

'How dreadful!' cried Laura piously. 'I have never heard anything like it!'

But Alice received the news quite calmly. She knew that the hot climates of the colonies were apt to have a deplorable effect on moral standards. 'It would explain why my mother always behaved with such tender con-

17

sideration towards Betty-Lou,' she said, raising candid eyes to Sir Geoffrey's.

'Well, Betty-Lou's claim to the plantation,' he explained with disastrous clarity, 'as eldest natural daughter of your grandfather, may be greater than your claim as natural daughter of your mother. I do not know. Mr Sellop was undecided about it. It is a trifling affair compared to the Lacey inheritance.'

'And totally unfit for discussion among well-brought-up females,' agreed Laura Lacey. 'Really—the scandal! I dread to think what our friends will say. Clara! Did I not tell you to leave the room?'

But Clara was not going to be moved. For once, real life was unfolding like a French novel.

'Betty-Lou,' breathed Alice. 'All this time . . .' It explained so much. No wonder the old woman was so jealous of Alice's jewelry. To her mind, those jewels should have been hers. Why had Alice taken so little notice of her senile grumblings? 'How did all this come to light?' she asked.

'Betty-Lou came to me towards the end of last year,' Geoffrey explained. 'She told me that your mother had never married my father during all the years that she had been her confidential maid.'

'And you listened to servants' gossip? Geoffrey, for shame!'

He flushed. 'She was very positive about it,' he said, 'and she should know. After all, she was in closest association with your mother while my own mother was still alive in England, and she came to Holt Lacey with your mother. She was with her all the time. It seems she has had a growing feeling of injustice for years and could no longer repress her claim to the Lestrange inheritance, particularly the family jewels.'

'But she is so old—she is more than a little mad. You cannot trust her word.'

'I took her to Mr Sellop. He questioned her closely and then sent to Nevis, as I told you. There is no

18

record of your mother's marriage there or in England after she came here with my father.'

'And you have known this for months and months and *never told me?*'

'Only suspected. Mr Sellop is a careful man, and did not consider the matter settled until today.'

Which explained why Geoffrey had not lifted a finger to check Laura's encroaching greed. 'Did you know?' Alice turned on her sister-in-law. But she did not need her denial to complete the picture. Geoffrey had known, and Geoffrey had been confident for weeks that all Alice possessed was his own.

'You should have told me,' Alice cried. It hurt. She had been so proud of her independence in handling the Lacey affairs—and now to learn all this had been going on behind her back. 'I ought to have known.'

'If you had known, you couldn't have gone on being so high-handed, could you?' asked Laura tartly. 'Having your own way about everything, when all the time it all belonged to us.'

Alice shook her head as though a gnat were buzzing round her. 'I must see Mr Sellop, Geoffrey,' she said. 'You must let me consult him. It is only fair.'

Her brother hesitated. 'Very well,' he said. 'I will take you to see him.'

Alice rose. 'I think I will go to bed now,' she said.

They did not try to stop her. They were avid to discuss the great good fortune that had come their way.

CHAPTER TWO

Alice passed a restless night and woke feeling sick and wretched. When she got out of bed, her head ached so abominably that the room blurred before her eyes and she was forced to lie down again. She rang for Mary, but she rang in vain. After about an hour, a small maid from the kitchen, whose name Alice barely knew, scratched on the door and timidly came in.

'If you please, Miss, Her Ladyship says you are late for breakfast.'

'Where is Mary?'

The small chit cast her eyes about nervously. 'If you please, Miss, Mary's not to be your maid no more, Miss. She's to help Frances in the drawing room and see to Miss Clara's hair.'

Alice stared dully. So Laura was not letting any grass grow under her feet! How cruel to publish Alice's changed status in the household so quickly. Hardly twelve hours since the news had broken!

'Tell Lady Lacey that I find myself unwell this morning and would like to breakfast in my room.'

After an hour and a half, the same small maid brought up a tray with some cold food on it, and Alice tried to force herself to eat.

For the rest of the day she was left severely alone. No-one sent any messages and no-one enquired after her health. Small muffled sounds came to her from time to time of quite feverish activities taking place beyond her door, and she could guess that Laura was taking enjoyable charge of the household and spreading the good news among her friends as rapidly as she could. Alice was thankful to be spared all this, but she began to realize that if she was to be cut out in future of the normal daily round of friends and plans and chats and calls and excursions, her life would become very bleak indeed. For what remained? A lonely existence with no occupation to fill it—neither mistress nor servant nor guest. How did poor relations, she now wondered, fill up their time?

Her fire was unmade. The ashes from last night lay idly on the dusty hearth and no neat housemaid appeared with fresh coals. Alice stayed in bed for warmth, and her shivering fits were due perhaps more to shock than cold, although it was the coolest spring that London had known for years.

Then gradually her natural good sense, good health and good humour began to come to the surface again.

Very well, she was poor, she was powerless, she had no prospects—but was that the end of everything? Her brother could not cast her out into the streets. He valued his name too well for that. She was simply in the position of countless other young ladies with no fortunes, pretty faces and fond hopes of finding a husband to support them for the rest of their lives.

Alice wrinkled her nose distastefully. She was not averse to matrimony, but she had calmly looked forward to bringing to her husband some large and welcome addition to his income. It is not only more blessed to give than to receive, it is also much more agreeable.

She pulled herself together. Regrets were not going to help. So, she must try to think clearly . . . from being one of the great catches of the Season, she had become yet another minnow in the marriage pool. Was that so terrible? She was no worse off than a hundred other young ladies who were gracing the ballrooms at this very time. No worse off than Clara Brown. Better, in fact, for though natural politeness would never allow her to say so, Alice knew perfectly well that Clara's pretty face could not hold a candle to her own dark, upstanding beauty. And Alice was an excellent hostess who had been running a large household since her mother's death and latterly quite on her own.

But Clara had been born in legal wedlock, and Alice's birth was clouded in ignominy and shame! What man who was seeking a beautiful and capable wife to grace the head of his table would overlook such a dreadful stain as that?

'Mama! Mama!' Alice buried her face in the pillow. 'How could you do this to me?' And into her mind came again the picture of that gentle, pious lady with the golden cross on her bosom, her voice softly raised as she read evening prayers to the assembled household. Alice lifted her head and frowned. Any connection between that figure and illicit passion was more than strange; it was incredible. And yet Geoffrey had been so sure . . .

'Papa,' wailed Alice, 'why were you so cruel?' And here Alice found no difficulty in believing Geoffrey's accusations. For no-one had been more likely to behave in a way that flouted moral convention than incorrigible, delightful Sir Walter Lacey. His vivid face with the wickedly glancing eyes flashed back into his daughter's mind unchanged. Although his clothes had become darker through her childhood, following the more sombre trend in fashions, he clung to bright waistcoats to the end and maintained, somehow, an air that hinted of red-lined cloaks and tricorne hats. How impulsive he had been—how patently in need of a careful wife's protection! No-one had been more remorseful after each one of his many lapses, or more likely to sin again. And no-one understood this better than his devoted daughter. It was one of the reasons she had adored him.

Evening brought dinner on a tray for Alice and a message by the same small maid that Her Ladyship trusted Miss Lestrange did not find herself indisposed. The meal in fact went a long way to restoring Alice. She brushed out her shining dark hair and washed her face in the stale, cold water that still stood on the marble-topped stand, and when the maid came back for the

23

tray, she found Alice in a long plum-coloured velvet wrapper with wide satin bands circling the shoulders and meeting at the back in a large satin bow.

'Please bring some coals,' said Alice crisply, 'and light my fire.'

Again a long, long wait. Alice's senses were fully alert now, and she could hear what was happening in the house outside her room. The carriage was waiting at the door—oh yes, of course. They had been invited by the Wyatts to a reception tonight, and Sir Geoffrey was to leave the House of Commons early to accompany his wife, for old Wyatt had much influence in the party.

Alice could hear the scurryings as Mary was sent down for hotter curling irons to crimp the little fizzy clusters which Clara affected behind her ears, and Laura's maid searched frantically for something left behind in the drawing-room—perhaps her smelling salts.

They would be the very centre of attraction at the reception tonight, thought Alice wrily. Everybody would crowd round to hear the extraordinary news, exclaim, congratulate and admire. How delighted their intimate friends would be!

And how chagrined would one or two gentlemen be at the loss of Alice! She smiled suddenly, and then laughed outright in release from the oppression of the day. How Charles Longford would regret the hours he had spent in pursuit of her with a volume of poems and a chestful of windy sighs. His bloodhound eyes would take on a mournful look that was genuine, for once. The pompous bore! And young Lord Locke with his grandfather's debts still unpaid and a string of younger brothers—how his blank eyes would open in that expressionless face when he heard that Miss Lacey was no longer worth his conscientious attentions. He had always believed that his moral worth would in the end wear down the resistance of such a well-brought-up young lady as Alice. And Captain the Honourable David Wargate, that handsome, devil-may-care (and impecunious) younger son—well, at least he had appeared to enjoy his energetic pursuit of her, and she hoped a touch of regret would droop the corners of that full-lipped mouth before he turned to other wealthy prey. What a let-down for all her suitors! Their faces would be a picture.

But Alice's own face soon fell. There were others whose company it would not be so delightful to lose. There were attentions which had been becoming apparent—perhaps only to her—but which had not been unwelcome. There was one gentleman who—who—Alice gripped her hands hard—who *could not* from his circumstances connect himself with a girl who had no fortune, but, worse than that, a stain across her birth.

Silently, bringing her hands to her mouth, Alice began to weep.

There came a knock at the door. Alice had been standing in the darkness, her room lit only by a glow from the window where a lamplighter had lit a street lamp an hour before. Now three forms hurried in, one carrying a branch of candles and another a wine glass and a decanter.

'Oh, Miss Alice!'

'My dear, be brave.'

'Oh Miss, they won't let me look after you any more. However are you going to put your hair up all by yourself then?'

The Lacey carriage had left, and the three most devoted of Alice's staff had lost no time in rushing in to comfort her. Mary, her maid, with her little round face alight with sympathy under its frilly cap, Frances, the gaunt chief parlourmaid and plump, grey-haired Mrs Vesey who had been Alice's housekeeper for many years, crowded round with little loving words of affection.

'Her Ladyship's not got the right to treat you so, Miss,' cried Frances. 'After you being so kind to her and giving Miss Clara so many nice things and all.'

'Dear Miss Alice, drink this,' Mrs Vesey pressed a glass

25

upon her. 'It is the very best port, and Dr Matthews always recommended it for the shock.'

'Thank you, thank you, Mrs Vesey.' Alice kissed her and buried her nose in the wine glass. It was harder to maintain self-control under all this sympathy than when she was on her own.

'Her Ladyship's talking of bringing in a page with buttons,' Frances told her gloomily. 'As if all these men about the place didn't cause nothing but trouble. That James! I've always been good enough to carry your messages without no mistakes, haven't I, Miss?'

'Run and bring a shovelful of hot coals from the drawing-room,' Mrs Vesey told Mary. 'And sweep up the hearth, Frances. Dear, dear, you're starved from cold, Miss Alice.' Mrs Vesey set about with her own hands to put the room in order, bang the feather pillows into shape and straighten the bed. In a few minutes the place was warm, a hot drink had been fetched and promises of continued love and service had been given by Alice's former staff which brought colour back to her cheeks and some sparkle to her eyes.

'I'll slip up and bring your hot water and do your hair each morning while they has breakfast below stairs, Miss,' Mary suggested before she left. 'That'll still give me time for Miss Clara. And I can change you for the evening before the others leave the drawing-room, if you would be so good as to come along here a little early.' She took out a clean white nightgown from the press, opened it and laid it carefully on the bed with her usual reverent expression. Mary knew nothing about the rights or wrongs of the Lacey inheritance, but she knew how to treat lace that had cost twenty-five shillings a yard!

'Would it be convenient if I got you ready for the night now, Miss?' she asked in her normal way.

Next morning, Alice got up early, determined to come

26

to terms with her new way of life. She would have, she felt, to make herself independent in spite of Mary's kind offers. Laura would not deal kindly with the servants who still favoured Alice. (Indeed, Frances was dismissed before the month was out.)

In her wrapper, before the mirror, Alice wrestled with the waist-long curtain of her hair. This Season it had been worn off the face, drawn back into a huge bun from which one long curl escaped to lie upon her shoulder. Many ladies had to pad their buns out with a chignon, but Alice had never needed one and this made her thankful now, for the task seemed impossible without added complications. Her cheeks became pink and her eyes angry as she wrestled with the warm, slippery masses, and in the end she tied it all back at the nape of her neck and twisted up a loose bun as best she could.

Alice selected a suitably sober grey gown from her bright stock, stepped into it, and found she was quite unable to complete her toilette. The dress was fastened from the nape of the neck to below the back of the waist with thirty-six tiny hooks and eyes. No matter how her slim body twisted and squirmed, it was a physical impossibility to fasten it up herself.

By breakfast time she was thoroughly chastened to find how difficult it would be to be a lady without a lady's maid to depend upon. The problem was not insoluble. There were, Alice knew, unfortunate ladies who could not afford a personal maid. They managed, and now Alice must learn to manage herself.

'I will not become shabby and untidy,' she promised herself fiercely as she left her room and walked towards the great staircase. 'Even if I have to earn my own bread. I suppose I could become a companion or a governess—thank heaven my dear mama made me keep up my Italian and music.'

She went downstairs with her head held high, conscious of curious glances from a footman who was carrying a refilled tea-urn. She was a little late. The silver dishes on the sideboard in the dining-room with their loads of eggs, kidneys, ham, mutton-chops and kedgeree were already cooling, and toast crumbs littered the starched white damask tablecloth. Sir Geoffrey had almost finished his breakfast and was leaning back over the *Morning Post*.

Her eyes met those of the two ladies. Clara was sitting in Alice's normal place at Sir Geoffrey's right hand. When Alice owned the house, it had been a graceful gesture on her part to offer her brother the head of the table. She had never given place to Clara, however, whose long stay classed her as a member of the family. Now—surely—she was not to lose the position she had so pleasantly assumed. Her chin rose. She was still, after all, a daughter of the house. Laura was not going to strip her of every honour she had once held on account of her wealth. She must, she must stand up for herself.

'Are you not in my place, Clara?' she asked conversationally.

Laura and Clara exchanged quick glances.

'I would prefer you to sit on the other side now, Alice,' Laura said.

'Surely my age gives me rights over Clara?' asked Alice in pleasant tones.

'Clara is my sister,' said Laura, 'and for the time being a resident of my house.'

'Sir Geoffrey's house,' Alice reminded her, 'and I am Sir Geoffrey's sister.'

Lady Lacey's back stiffened. 'Alice!' she said sharply. 'Try not to be indelicate. And remember that you are not in law your papa's daughter at all. You reside in this house only by your bro—by Sir Geoffrey's generosity, and your "place", now that you mention it, does not exist.'

A cough and a rustle of the *Morning Post* showed that Sir Geoffrey was not going to interfere. Clara had the grace to drop her eyes, but she could not hide a little gleeful pleasure at the scene.

Alice sank into the empty chair with heightened colour. What a fool she had been to raise the question! What did it *matter* who sat where? How often she had laughed at the complicated rules that governed society —at the way married daughters hurried to take precedence over their unmarried sisters—at one ill-bred baronet's daughter who always pushed herself forward in front of her much worthier mother-in-law. It was all so petty and stupid.

And yet to the under-privileged, she now realized, such tiny pin-picks could give the most bitter hurts.

I won't knuckle under, she thought desperately. Laura can push me so far, but no further. Yet she is out to make my life impossible. There must be some means of escape.

'While we are on the subject,' went on Lady Lacey inexorably. 'Sir Geoffrey and I have discussed what your position in the house should be.'

Great heavens! They must have been working like coal-porters all yesterday, thought Alice, amused in spite of herself.

'You will not now, of course, expect to dine with us when we have company,' her sister-in-law went on. 'Though our friends are as liberal as we are ourselves towards the unfortunate, we cannot ask them to meet someone whom they would not allow their daughters to know.'

Alice gasped. 'Geoffrey . . .?' she cried in unbelieving tones.

The head of the household escaped with a few muttered words about 'committee' and 'House' and a brief farewell peck at his wife's forehead. Clara rose and excused herself. Laura graciously let her go. 'Come to me in my little sitting-room in an hour, my love,' she told her sister, 'and the carriage will be waiting to take us to pay calls.'

Alice had turned quite white. *Her* carriage! *Her* little downstairs sitting-room where she kept all her own cherished possessions and her beloved mother's things. But what were these trifles compared with the dart that Laura had planted so cruelly—that Alice had become a person from whom young ladies should be carefully shielded? Alice could not believe that this was true.

'We have decided, Sir Geoffrey and I,' went on Lady Lacey, 'that although it would not be suitable for you to be present at evening parties, it would be cruel,' she smiled sweetly, 'to deprive you of all social intercourse, brought up as you have been. You will be expected to attend when my friends take tea with me and when I have morning callers—ladies of established position who would not find your presence an embarrassment.'

Alice understood it all. Her party days were obviously over. But Laura was not going to allow this nine-days-wonder Alice Lacey (no, Alice *Lestrange*), once great heiress, now dependent on charity, to hide herself away from all the gossip-mongers of the town. Whilst the news was at its height, while all the tongues were tattling about her, she was to be dragged out and exhibited to Laura's particular friends.

'I would prefer,' she said, with stony quiet, 'to remain in my room when you have company.'

'Yes, but what you prefer, my dear Alice, has very little to do with the case. You will do what I require in the future.' And having made her point, underlined it, dotted the i's and crossed the t's, Lady Lacey rose and sailed out of the room.

Somehow Alice managed to get upstairs with her head held proudly. The house seemed full of inquisitive and unfriendly eyes. The footman at the door and two housemaids coming out of the drawing-room gave her a taste of the malicious glances and whisperings she was going to encounter everywhere. These were London staff, employed by Alice only for the Season when the town house was in use. She reached her room dry-eyed but with the colour high in her cheeks.

'I've lit the fire, Miss, and done the room and there's plenty of coals in the scuttles if you would be so good as to put them on yourself, Miss,' whispered Frances, who had been waiting for her.

'Oh bless you!' cried Alice, giving her former parlour-maid a hug, but as soon as the door had closed behind the maid, she burst into tears.

CHAPTER THREE

This would not do. Alice pulled herself together. If she allowed Laura to depress her so sadly, she would soon turn into one of those dim, tremulous figures that hovered in the background of their richer relatives' lives, depressingly grateful for the smallest crumb of attention. Alice made a tremendous resolution to find out whether she was in fact the owner of Frenchman's Point Plantation on the island of Nevis in the West Indies, and, if she were, to go there and live in however small a way. If not, she must get away from the Laceys. Surely some of her former acquaintances would raise a hand to help her?

In the meantime, she must try to make life simpler to suit her new condition. Alice went to the closet that held her clothes and came back with an armful of dresses which she flung on the bed. She had been most particular when they had been made about the cut, the line and the fitting. It had never occurred to her to consider whether they were easy to put on or not.

She found that her ball-gowns, for the main, were fastened at the back so that nothing would interrupt the lavish trimming over the low bosom. Many day dresses, however, were in the new fashion; hooked up to a high neck in front. The openings were concealed in various ways, with strips of lace, tucks or cleverly placed braid. One walking dress, of which Alice was particularly fond, fastened with gilt buttons from the centre of the waist to the shoulder. A row of mock buttons to the other shoulder balanced the opening and created a very chic effect.

Alice examined it carefully. It was a frivolous garment. Long gold fringes edged the pagoda sleeves and a crossed pattern of gold braid formed a wide decorative

33

band round the hem. But the basic material was good brown wool muslin, and were there not rows of plain brown buttons on that riding coat she so disliked . . . ? Alice took her needlecase from a drawer, picked up a pair of gold-mounted manicure scissors and tackled the gold trimmings which were no longer suitable to her situation in life.

Mary brought her lunch on a tray, 'seeing as how Her Ladyship's not returned for hers, Miss,' and Alice mumbled her thanks through a mouthful of pins. For the first time in her life she blessed those impatient hours she had spent as a small girl reluctantly stitching samplers.

At four o'clock she stood up and stretched and flexed her cramped fingers. Three highly respectable plain gowns lay across the bed, one brown, one black and one of chaste pearl grey, and a huge pile of lace, bright braid and colourful trimmings littered the floor. Alice was moderately pleased with herself, but very stiff and weary. 'A ride would be delightful,' she thought and her hand went to the bell, then stopped. No doubt her horses now belonged to her brother and Laura. She winced. How pleasant that life had been, the one she led before!

Alice walked up and down her room to get the blood back into her limbs. There were several things which it behoved her to do without loss of time, and the first one, she thought, would be to write to her godmother, Mrs Gorman. The old lady was completely unpredictable, and might well drop Alice like a hot brick, but on the other hand she could be a warm-hearted friend if she chose. And Alice needed friends very badly.

She went downstairs to the small sitting-room where her writing materials were kept and gasped as she opened the door. Laura was seated at her desk and all Alice's papers were spread around her. Her letters had been taken out of their little tied packets and were heaped in an untidy pile. Her book of engagements

34

already showed entries in Laura's handwriting. Alice's engraved visiting cards had been dropped into the waste basket, and her meticulously kept account books were lying higgledy-piggledy about the floor.

But, worst of all, from the walls and tables around Alice's desk, the portrait of her mother had been lifted and thrown face downwards on to the sofa and her mother's carved crucifix had been cast on top of it, together with the little icon that had stood in triple-pointed elegance on a walnut table and the carved rosary which had lain in front of it.

'You may carry these things away, Alice, if they have any value to you,' Laura informed her briskly.

'May I have some writing-paper, please, Laura?' asked Alice after swallowing to keep her emotions under control.

Laura looked at her enquiringly. Surely, thought Alice acidly, she doesn't think I lost the power to write as soon as I lost my name?

'I wish to tell my godmother what has happened to me,' Alice was forced to explain, 'and also to put off my mother's cousin, who was to have come on a visit. You will not want her to come now, I imagine?'

'You are quite right to cancel any arrangements you made in the past,' Laura agreed, 'and those letters should go. But in future you cannot expect Sir Geoffrey to frank your mail as he has done before. You will have to rely on the penny post.' Her head went back to the desk and Alice felt dismissed. As she gathered her things up, she could see that Laura was writing out invitation cards, and wondered whether the party she was planning was to be a big one. She wondered if Laura had any idea what such parties cost? The abandoned ledgers seemed to indicate that Lady Lacey had not been used to enquiring very closely into how the household books were balanced, and Alice had no knowledge of how the Laceys managed in their own home. Her fingers itched for a hand in the arrange-

35

ments. These London servants could run away with a fortune if they were not constantly checked, and Mrs Vesey was not strong-minded enough to keep the cooks properly under control. But it had nothing to do with her now.

'Laura, how am I to take exercise?' she asked. 'Presumably you do not want me to go riding with Clara?'

Lady Lacey put the tip of her pen to her teeth and considered. She had given up riding herself as soon as she married and her figure had started to show the lack of it. 'You may go walking in the park, Alice,' she said. 'I have often seen nursemaids and governesses congregating near the pond.'

Alice flushed. 'It would not be seemly for me to walk through the streets alone,' she said. 'May I take a maid to go with me?'

'Not Mary,' Laura replied immediately. 'Mary is not to be considered your maid any more, Alice. But I will tell Mrs Vesey that one of the other maids can go with you—unless it hinders the work in the kitchen, of course.'

The bitter reply that had risen to Alice's tongue was kept back by the entry of a slim young man who came into the room in a hurry and then stopped short when he saw Alice.

Percy Brown, Laura's brother, was a handsome young barrister who was neglecting his legal career in an attempt to make his name in the House of Commons. Percy was of the same fair complexion as his two sisters, but in his case the blond hair was more sandy than yellow, and his whiskers had a distinctly reddish tinge. It had been Laura's dearest wish that he should make himself independent by marrying Alice Lacey, and every effort that she could make had previously been channelled into this desirable plan, each such effort being steadily opposed by Alice.

Now Laura sprang from her chair and was for the moment left without a word at her command.

Percy Brown came slowly across the room. 'Miss Lacey!' he exclaimed. She bowed her head slightly and he coloured. 'I mean—er—' It was difficult. What was he to call her now? 'Allow me to give you my sincere condolences, Miss—er—Miss Alice,' he said feelingly. 'This news must have caused you the deepest distress.'

Alice gave him a brief smile. She had never been quite sure how far Percy Brown's intentions had fallen in with those of his sister, but she was thankful to find now that his manners were much kinder and more thoughtful than those of Laura had been.

'That will be all, Alice,' said Lady Lacey hastily, but Alice was already leaving the room.

The days passed in agonizing slowness. If Alice had been asked before, she would have said that the spring months spent in London away from her normal duties in the country had been a holiday, an enjoyable waste of time. She now realized that the daily ride in the park, the morning calls, the visits to the shops, seamstresses and mantle-makers and the informal tea-taking that took place before the round of balls and parties, which had been the really important part of her London life, had crammed every minute of the day in a very satisfactory manner. Take them and the running of the house away and there was nothing left. She began to think she must perforce become a governess to have something to do.

Her brother was as good as his word and did arrange an interview with the family attorney. He drove Alice down to the office in Mount Street to see Mr Sellop, a grey-haired figure with the pallid face of a man who spent all his days among his dusty deeds and documents. He took her hand in great sorrow and peered into her eyes with great concern and introduced her to a much younger solicitor who showed signs of exposure to the sun.

'This is Mr Christopher,' explained Mr Sellop, 'who went on our behalf to the West Indies to make the enquiries about your mother. He is not a member of our firm, but I can assure you that he performed his duties conscientiously.'

Alice bowed.

'You wish to question me, my dear, about the outcome of these regrettable discoveries,' said the old lawyer, seating Alice in the most comfortable chair. 'And I would like to express my own personal surprise —nay, dismay—at what has been disclosed. I cannot understand why Sir Walter behaved as he did. It is perfectly extraordinary. Tell me, Miss—er—Miss Alice, did your mother ever give the slightest hint that she had contracted a previous marriage, perhaps? That a former husband was alive—had long deserted her? Such an occurrence would have, of course, prevented Sir Walter and she from a legal union.'

'No. No. The very opposite was the case. My father visited Nevis many years before my mother came to England. They fell in love then and were most anxious to get married. But my grandpapa, old Mr Lestrange, would not permit it because Sir Walter was not a Catholic as my mother was. It almost broke her heart. Sir Walter came back to England and married Geoffrey's mother, and my own mother nearly pined away. But as soon as Sir Walter's wife had died, he came straight over to Nevis and married her.'

'A very romantic tale,' said Mr Sellop, sadly shaking his head. 'And it fits with every particular which I had previously understood. I take it you got these facts from your mother, my dear?'

'Oh no. She was extremely reticent about her personal affairs.'

'Then from your father?'

'No. You remember my father, Mr Sellop, he always lived in the present, not the past.'

'Yes indeed. Then who told you your mother's story?'

'Her maid,' said Alice, suddenly biting her lip.

'Betty-Lou?'

38

'Yes. Betty-Lou.'

'She had been with your mother all the time and knew every detail of the story?'

'Yes. No. That is, I believe Betty-Lou was banished to St Kitts, the neighbouring island, for several years and was not present when Sir Walter came to Nevis for the first time. When she returned she found my mother much changed, so quiet and sad. All the servants on the plantation knew what had happened and told her that my grandfather had forbidden the wedding. I believe Betty-Lou nursed my mother through a dangerous illness about that time.'

'Your grandfather was not alive when the marriage is supposed to have taken place . . . let me see, the year Sir Walter visited the West Indies for the second time . . . where is it? Ah yes, 1840?'

'No. He died a few months before.'

'It is very strange,' repeated the old lawyer. 'Most odd. I have never come across a case quite like it before. You are sure, my dear, that your mother could not have contracted some other alliance—a thoroughly unsuccessful one—during the years that Sir Walter himself was married in England?'

'How can I know?' asked Alice a little wildly. 'I wasn't there. And does it really matter, Mr Sellop, if you have other means of demonstrating your case?'

'It would establish your legitimate birth, my dear,' said Mr Sellop in mild reproof, 'in law. Although nobody doubts you are in fact Sir Walter's daughter. And it would provide a satisfactory explanation for their otherwise incomprehensible behaviour.'

'Oh.'

'I think I should say,' cut in the young attorney, blushing as he addressed Alice, 'that I talked to many old workers at Frenchman's Point who remembered your mother well. The point came up, and they were convinced that your mother never considered marriage with any other man after Sir Walter left the island. She withdrew from society and devoted a great deal of her life to religion and prayer.'

'Are you satisfied now, Alice?' asked Geoffrey. 'Because I have other calls upon my time.'

'Oh no, please, Geoffrey. I have barely begun. Mr Sellop, when this matter first came up, why did you believe the word of Betty-Lou? She has been touchy and unreliable for years. I have never been able to manage her as my mother did. Why did you not send her off as a trouble-maker?'

'My dear Miss Alice,' said Mr Sellop earnestly. 'We took the story as pure fabrication at first. It just happened that I had decided to send Mr Christopher to Nevis in any case to look into the reason why the plantation was producing such poor results, and as Betty-Lou was so importunate, I asked him—that is Sir Geoffrey and I asked him—to get concrete evidence of your parents' marriage simply to silence the woman. We never expected that she might be speaking the truth until the first letters came.'

'And how can you know that the record of my mother's marriage is not lying somewhere unknown to you—that Betty-Lou did not know where the ceremony had taken place?'

'Indeed, indeed, Miss Alice,' the old man was quite distressed. 'Do not think we have left any stone unturned. I am only anxious to serve the Lacey family as my father did before me, and at that time I merely wanted to confirm the terms of your father's will. Mr Christopher examined all the parish registers on Nevis for the year 1840—and beyond, I believe—and when he drew a blank there, we still took it for granted that the marriage had taken place in England after your mother's arrival. But this was not so. There are plenty of witnesses who can recall your mother's reception at Holt Lacey. She came as Lady Lacey, was introduced everywhere as Lady Lacey and, as your birth followed within a year of her arrival, she lived very quietly at home. The steward will swear that she never went beyond the manor park gates for over a year after coming to England, and very seldom after that.'

This rang true. Alice remembered her mother as almost entirely confined to the house and the park, except for Sunday Mass. It was Alice who, as she got older, had ridden far over the estate in the company of her father. 'Where did my mother land on her arrival in England?' she asked.

'At Bristol. They were met by the Lacey carriage and brought straight to Holt Lacey.'

'Oh. There was no question, then, of her being married in the city?'

'We have searched the records there, Miss Alice,' said the young attorney. 'We have looked in every parish register for miles around Holt Lacey. They might possibly have been married some years later further afield, but no marriage took place before your birth.'

'I shall ask Mrs Vesey . . .' Alice said slowly. But she knew it was no use. The housekeeper would have been the first to rush forward with evidence if she had known of any.

'I trust you are satisfied now, Alice,' said Sir Geoffrey rising. 'I will take you home.'

'No, Geoffrey. Please give me a little longer.'

Her brother clucked impatiently, but Alice was giving the old attorney a long considering look. She had dropped any suspicion that had fluttered in her mind that the whole affair might be a conspiracy between her brother and the man of law. Mr Sellop was too much a part of her youth, he had always shown a partiality to her on his brief visits to the West Country, and she did not doubt him when he said his one wish was to serve the Lacey family interests.

'Mr Sellop,' she said. 'My father must have *known* that he was not married to my mother. So why did he refer to me as *Alice Lacey* in his will?'

41

The old man shrugged. 'To spare your mother's memory, perhaps. No man wants to publish his old sins before the world.'

'I should like to go now, Alice,' said her brother.

'Wait, Geoffrey, *please*. Mr Sellop, my father was no fool. And he really wanted me to inherit the Lacey lands, didn't he?'

'Indeed he did. I tried to reason with him. I will not conceal from you, Miss Alice, that I thought he was showing—er—excessive favouritism in the distribution of his property, but the will was worded exactly as he wished.'

'Then why ever did he write my name as Alice *Lacey*?' demanded Alice. 'If he had put *my daughter Alice*, would that not have been sufficient?'

'Indeed it would. He did not specify in the case of Sir Geoffrey here. "I leave to my son Geoffrey . . ." he put in the normal fashion.'

'And all this trouble has come to be because he put that one word in his will?' cried Alice, scarcely able to believe it. 'Oh Papa!'

'There would still be the question of the legitimacy,' said the old lawyer prudently, but Alice was not interested. She was marvelling at behaviour so entirely out of keeping with the indulgent parent that she remembered.

'I cannot wait any longer Alice,' said Geoffrey angrily.

Alice was forced to rise. 'Mr Sellop,' she said, 'I take it unkindly that I was left so long in the dark about this. I should have been informed the moment a doubt was raised.'

He took her hand and pressed it affectionately. 'We hoped you would never hear of it, my dear,' he said. 'It seemed like a small cloud that would soon blow over. I never thought . . . alas!' And he shook his head regretfully.

Sir Geoffrey opened the door for Alice.

'But even if the matter were brought to court,' went

42

on the old attorney, 'I cannot see but that the result would be the same.'

'What did he mean?' asked Alice, turning her head as she climbed into the carriage. ' "If the matter were brought to court"? Is this something that should be decided by a judge, Geoffrey?'

'Of course not,' said her brother, banging on the floor of the carriage so loudly with his stick that the coachman whipped the horses up. 'You have heard all the evidence yourself. Everything that could be done on your behalf has been done, and at great cost, which I shall have to meet myself. You should be completely satisfied.'

'But I had no chance to ask whether the Frenchman's Point Plantation belongs to me or to Betty-Lou. I should like to consult Mr Sellop again, Geoffrey.'

'That is out of the question. Ladies should not deal directly with attorneys. Their minds are unsuited to it.'

'Nevertheless, I should like to.' Mr Sellop's closing remarks had started up several trains of thought in Alice's mind.

'And I have decided, my dear Alice, that you shall not. You can communicate with him in writing. I will grant you that grace. You may give your letters to me, unsealed, and if I approve of them, I will pass them on.'

A helpless, hopeless, stultifying pall of frustration came down slowly upon Alice's head. What chance did she have of getting her own way? None. Her brother could rule her life as absolutely as if she were a kitchen maid—more absolutely. Wealth had given her an independence highly unusual for a female and now it was gone. She could barely call her soul her own.

Her first introduction to society came when the wives of some Members of Parliament took tea with Lady Lacey one evening when their husbands were expected to sit late in the House. It was an ordeal for which she had prepared herself in the tiny attic room she now occupied. Smooth hair, plain dress, small onyx pin—one of the few pieces of jewelry that Laura had left her.

She took a seat at the far end of the drawing-room between two heavy falls of curtain and half hidden behind a huge palm tree in a Chinese pot which had been one of Laura's recent lavish purchases. If the visitors did not want to know her, they could pretend that they had not seen her there. And as the ladies entered, they greeted Laura and Clara and gathered round the fire, and Alice was not quite sure whether she had been observed or not. However, Lady Arthur swept across the room immediately and took Alice by the arms.

'My dear,' she cried. 'You are looking pale. And who can wonder? What a terrible thing to have happened to you. How could your dear papa have behaved so badly? It gives me great pain to see you suffer so.'

This was a comfort, for Lord Arthur was Comptroller of India and a powerful voice in the government, and his wife's attention could only give Alice consequence. She stayed by the girl's side for some time and several ladies who had hung back before came forward to pay their stiff respects. Not all. Alice could hear the Countess of Mark say to Laura in a barely subdued voice that she was 'surprised the gel was admitted to the society of decent people', and other ladies who would normally have fawned on Alice now turned their backs.

Surprise and bustle took over when the gentlemen began pouring into the room. The parliamentary business had been completed early and Sir Geoffrey had brought his friends along to join their wives. Alice found herself the object of the attention of a middle-aged man whom she barely knew.

'My dear Miss Alice,' he declared, working away at her hand as though it were a pump handle. 'This is a calamity indeed! The sins of the father have been visited on an innocent child. What a terrible lesson for

44

all of us! My sister and I were shocked to hear about it.'

'You are very kind, Mr Bunne,' she said, gently releasing herself.

'But you will have the fortitude to bear it,' he assured her with a myopic peer. 'I said to Letitia, "The Lord will support the young lady's steps along the strait and narrow way," I said, "You see if He don't. She has the look of one with great moral purpose and pious intent." '

Alice smiled at this representation of herself and was grateful for the kindness. Mr Bunne was a good, prosy sort of man who had held a small post in the late government and his sister was known to be an ardent Methodist. He continued at some length to produce biblical examples of strength in trying circumstances and she continued, politely, to express her gratitude.

John Gorman, who sat on the Treasury Bench with Sir Geoffrey and who was one of his particular cronies, also came straight to Alice's side. She was surprised and pleased, for she had doubted if he would remain her friend. 'Violet sends her dearest love,' he said, 'and wishes you to come for a long stay when she is fully recovered.'

'Give her my love,' said Alice, blinking back tears, 'and of course my best wishes for her safe delivery.'

'Have you heard from my mother?'

'No. I was surprised. I wrote to Godmama some time ago, but there has been no reply at all.'

'Well,' he grimaced, 'she is a law unto herself, but I would not expect her to desert you. Forgive me, Alice, but I promised Violet I would return as soon as I was free. What a crowd is here tonight! Excuse me, Locke, am I in your way?'

But Lord Locke turned a rigid back and rapidly retreated. He had no wish to give the impression that his former attentions to Alice were to continue.

45

She hung her head, more moved by evidence of kindness than she had been by harsh suppression.

'Miss Alice,' said a quiet voice. London seemed to have hit on this new title for her, halfway, as it were, between Miss Lacey and Miss Lestrange.

Alice looked up. Mr Matthew Vale was standing quite close beside her. The famous black brows that sent shivers of delicious fright through every young innocent heart in London were drawn together in their masterful way, and the blue eyes beneath them were examining her intently. Against her will, Alice blushed. 'Mr Vale,' she acknowledged as steadily as she could. It was as well to get the worst over quickly. But why had he not turned his back on her like Lord Locke? Surely that would have been easier for both of them?

'I asked after you when I called a few days ago,' Matthew Vale went on gravely, 'but Lady Lacey said you were unavailable. I trust that you have not been unwell?'

'Quite well, thank you, Mr Vale,' Alice replied formally. There was a pause, and Alice held her breath. This was the greatest trial of all. She *must* behave naturally. Above all, she must not attract attention to the man—his height and commanding presence were usually enough to do that on their own. He had been kind to speak to her at all. Let that be enough. But forced to stand close together in the crowded room, the curve of her drably-clad bosom was only inches away from the muscular bulge of his arm under his very fashionable coat, and Alice struggled to hide her distress. Why did he not stand further away? Was it fair to either of them?

At their very first meeting that strong right arm had pulled Alice unceremoniously out of a muddy brook and dumped her on a slippery bank all golden with October leaves. Barely out of the schoolroom, it was her first venture into the hunting field, and she was shivering with fright from her horse's fall and desperately

46

conscious of her muddy wet riding habit and hair all over her shoulders. But worst of all she had *screamed* when the horse (a new present from her father) took the bit between its teeth and bolted across two fields, flying the hedges and launching itself from the very worst spot on the bank of the little stream.

Alice had hardly dared to come down to the hunt dinner that night and had cast her eyes low to avoid contemptuous glances—but it had been all right! Everyone was in the best of spirits after a splendid day, and everyone seemed to take it for granted that Alice had enjoyed herself too. 'Hear you took a toss, Alice,' her father called across the room. 'Vale said you were very brave, but that mare's too strong for you. We'll get rid of her.' No-one called her the miserable little coward she felt herself to be, and obviously no-one had heard about that involuntary, shame-making scream. And Alice, eyes happily raised now, had given silent thanks where she felt they were due. People might denounce Matthew Vale as a rake, but in her mind he was a perfect gentleman. He had saved her from scorn then, and she was anxious to save him from stray whispers now. He must leave her side—but no, he seemed determined to go on talking.

'If you will allow me to mention it,' he said, finding words with some difficulty, 'your friends have been deeply distressed to hear of your misfortune.'

She bowed her head.

'When blows of fate fall like this upon quite innocent people . . .' he began rather awkwardly, and stopped.

Alice gripped a tiny fold of her gown between two fingers. She had been told several times this evening that the Lord would give her the strength to bear her load cheerfully. 'If he mentions the shorn lamb, I shall *scream*,' she thought with pain.

'. . . then it behoves their friends to do everything they can to help. I should think it an honour, Miss Alice, if you would call on me in any way.'

This was handsome! As unexpected as it was welcome.

'You are very kind,' Alice said sincerely, raising flushed cheeks to him.

'It is the least I can do,' said Matthew Vale sadly, looking down into the lovely face.

He did not need to say more, for Alice understood what lay behind his words. If ever there was a man who was unable to marry poverty and low birth, that man was Matthew Vale! All thoughts of a tender relationship between them were dead—had to be dead. But in that moment Alice recognized as clearly as if he had spoken that Mr Vale had intended to ask her to be his wife. She dropped her eyes to hide the happiness that went with the despair.

'I trust that you will not cease to regard me as a friend,' he said, and there was so much truth in his voice that Alice could not let his offer pass.

'There is something . . .' she began.

'Yes?'

'Well, there are two things which I very much wish to discuss with Mr Sellop—the attorney.'

'I know old Sellop. He's a good man. Go on.'

'He said something in his office the other day which made me wonder . . . but Geoffrey has expressly forbidden me to consult him again.'

'Sir Geoffrey's commands have no power over me,' said Matthew Vale. 'Tell me what it is you wish to know.'

'Mr Sellop hinted,' said Alice, wrinkling her brows, 'that the question of my inheritance might be raised in court. Could you find out what he meant? I have been thinking that if the will has to come before a Judge in Chancery—or whatever it is that happens to wills— someone ought to be there to show how strongly my father *intended* for me to have the Lacey part of the property even though he called me by the wrong name. Or does that seem nonsensical to you?' she added hastily.

48

'Not at all. A very good point, I should have thought. I will see Sellop tomorrow and ask him myself. Lawyers are notoriously close-mouthed about their clients' affairs, but if the old man won't help us, we'll set another fellow on to it.'

'Oh no, Mr Vale, I cannot permit . . .'

'You are not required to permit anything, Miss Alice,' he replied calmly. Almost the same words as Geoffrey so frequently used nowadays. But these only brought warmth to her heart.

'And the second matter?' Matthew asked.

'It is about my mother's sugar plantation on the island of Nevis,' said Alice. 'It is a small, unprofitable affair, but at least I thought that would remain to me. Yet there is another claimant to it who seems to have a better right to it than I have.'

'Did your mother have another child?'

'No. It is a little difficult. There is a half-caste woman called Betty-Lou who was, she says, my grandfather's natural child. If I am only the natural child of my mother, she says she has a better claim.'

'Nonsense. Your mother inherited in the normal way, didn't she? And the inheritance passes automatically to her child. It doesn't go sideways.'

'But Geoffrey says that natural children do not have any right of inheritance in any way. He will not discuss it, but I believe he thinks that as my mother had no legal heir, the property would revert to the next heir of my grandpapa, who in default of anybody else would be Betty-Lou.'

'You mean the natural sister of a woman like your mother would have a greater claim to property than the natural daughter?' asked Matthew Vale, greatly intrigued. 'I can see . . .'

'Mr Vale,' said a voice over his shoulder in deep disapproval, 'is it fitting to discuss such subjects with a lady situated as Miss Alice is?' And Mr Bunne's short-sighted eyes gazed through their glasses in shocked dismay.

Alice blushed right up to the roots of her hair. How could she have so forgotten herself? To be talking in a drawing-room, quite casually and enjoyably, on subjects which a young lady should not even know exist? But that was the trouble with Mr Vale. He made every subject so natural and interesting.

'Perhaps you would prefer us to discuss the weather?' asked Matthew in bored tones. 'Let me start by saying it is inclement, and then you can point out that the crops are coming on fast.'

But Mr Bunne was not to be put off by pointed rudeness. He fastened himself to Alice's side and stood there like a plump St George in defence of purity. Matthew was forced to take his leave, but he promised Alice before he left that he would pursue the matter further.

Next morning at breakfast Lady Lacey displayed a touch of bad temper that had several causes. She had found that the world in which she moved was showing more sympathy to Alice than she thought necessary, and the leader of her husband's party had hinted that Laura's too obvious delight in her own sudden acquisition of houses, carriage and great wealth might be in bad taste.

'I shall be obliged, Alice, if you will not put yourself forward so much as you did last evening,' she said crossly.

Alice silently buttered toast. It would have been difficult to take a place further back in the drawing-room than her own had been.

'Our friends,' went on Laura, 'and particularly our gentlemen friends, do not wish to be dragged into conversation by young persons whose acquaintance can only be a matter of indifference to them. Am I not right, Geoffrey?'

'No doubt, my dear.' He was taking the letters from a silver tray.

50

'And Clara,' continued Her Ladyship, 'it is a complete waste of time to sit on a sofa and wait for people to come up to you. You should attach yourself to a group—unobtrusively of course—and then you will be drawn into the conversation.'

'I didn't want to talk to anybody last night,' said Clara sulkily. 'They were all too old.'

'You keep a civil tongue in your head, Miss,' said Laura, turning an anxious eye at her husband. With a little careful management, now that he was so very well off, Sir Geoffrey might be persuaded to provide for his sister-in-law if she would only behave prettily.

'A letter for you, Miss.' The butler brought his tray to Alice.

'How strange!' said Lady Lacey. 'A bill, no doubt. But Sir Geoffrey is taking responsibility for all the expenses you made so wrongfully in the past—you had better pass it to me, Alice.'

But Alice had already taken the letter, broken the seal, and opened a scrawled page of thick paper that was ever so lightly stained by damp at the edges.

'Great heavens!' she cried. 'What a calamity!'

'What is it?' asked Clara Brown.

Alice raised her head, eyes wide with dismay.

'Well?' demanded Lady Lacey.

'It is from Miss St George. She has already left St Kitts. "By the time this reaches you," she says, "I shall have boarded the next packet, and will look to be with you well before the end of the Season." She must have left before my note came, telling her not to sail.'

Sir Geoffrey laid down his mail, arrested by Alice's tone. 'Who is Miss St George?' he demanded.

'Marianne. Do you not recall her, Geoffrey?' replied Alice. 'My distant cousin on my mama's side of the family,' she added.

Laura and Clara were showing great signs of interest and consternation.

'The heiress from St Kitt's!' breathed Clara, and her eyes went round.

'Dear me . . . what are we to do about Miss St George?' wondered Laura aloud.

There was deep silence round the breakfast table. Sir Geoffrey was merely surprised. He had probably never been informed of the colonial orphan who was to visit London this summer. Alice did not know what to do, but she had to smile as she watched various emotions chase their way across Laura's face. She had banished Alice, socially speaking, and could banish this Miss St George by merely closing her doors. But was that wise treatment for a St Kitts heiress with no London friends?

A St Kitts heiress—it was a common enough phrase. It described any girl from the West Indies with a pile of sugar money. A general term, it conjured up pictures of great wealth, pampered constitutions and whining complaints about the British climate.

And here was a *real* heiress from the *real* St Kitts, and reliable news had foretold that her fortune was enormous and entirely at her own disposal. Laura's eyes grew calculating. One prosperous marriage had escaped her brother's grasp when Alice's bright future vanished. This would bring another one right into his orbit. A dependent, shy, sickly little hot-house plant from so enervating a background could be bent to Laura's will almost before she got her foot through the door into London society.

'Does Miss St George know what's happened to you?' Clara asked Alice naively.

'Of course not.' Laura turned on her sister. 'How could she, when the mails had not yet arrived?' She looked at Alice with an expression more acidly agreeable than any she had worn since she became mistress of the house. 'We can hardly turn Miss St George away when she was expressly invited,' she said. 'And especially since she is some sort of relative of our own. I shall allow your cousin to stay here while she is in London,

52

Alice. It will make no difference to your position, of course, but she can go out with me and Clara, and I expect you to feel grateful.'

Back in her small attic room, Alice considered what was likely to happen. She could remember the tiny creature who had been sent to England some ten years before to consult doctors, but that was no guide to the present. Marianne St George had then been a darting, bright-eyed, chatterbox of a body with a little pointed face and a mass of dark curls, full of hero-worship for her elder, more sedate cousin. Now she was an heiress and Alice was without a penny. 'No doubt she will feel it necessary to drop me as soon as she hears what has happened,' surmised Alice, biting her lip. 'I must make it easy for her.' Blood, being thicker than water, was also harder to wipe off.

But in the meantime the chill winds of fortune were blowing a little less keenly.

'Oh Miss,' Mary burst into her bedroom. 'Lady Lacey's compliments, and you have been specially asked to accompany Her Ladyship on a call on Lady Arthur. And Her Ladyship says I am to help you with your hair!'

CHAPTER FOUR

Although it was the hurricane season, nothing impeded the arrival of the ship from St Kitts, and about two weeks later, three hackney carriages and a large drag loaded with trunks and baskets arrived to create a tremendous bustle in the hall of the house at Portman Square.

Miss St George had come under the chaperonage of a respectable parson and his wife and large family, who were on their way to Cambridge, and who refused all offers of Lady Lacey's hospitality in their desire to make the journey in one day.

Alice stood hesitant at a curve of the staircase and watched the scene from above. Marianne St George presented only the top of a small white forward-tilting hat of daunting elegance and slim shoulders draped in a bright Spanish shawl. Her deep red skirts billowed out in the widest possible circumference, and nobody could guess, thought Alice, from this first glimpse that her clothes were provincial, let alone colonial.

She noticed that her cousin took mere formal leave of her clerical guards and that she curtsied deeply to Lady Lacey in a way that had gone out of fashion several years before.

'But where is Alice?' she heard her cry as soon as the visitors had left. Alice retreated up the stairs in front of Laura and Clara who were leading Marianne up to the drawing-room. This was going to be hard. As a child, Marianne had pattered after Alice like a devoted doll, and now she would be told that her cousin was unfit to befriend. Alice went ahead into the drawing-room, raised her chin and prepared for the worst.

'Alice!' cried a happy voice, and Miss St George raced

55

across the room and flung herself into her arms. 'But you have grown so tall!' she exclaimed, after kissing her friend warmly and revealing a very pretty face with the whitest skin Alice had ever seen. 'And you are so beautiful! So like your mama! Oh Alice, how I have longed —all these years—to be with you again. Isn't it lucky that grandpapa died so opportunely? It has been like a jail at Beauregarde for the last two or three years.'

Lady Lacey coughed. Marianne whirled round. 'Forgive me,' she said winningly. 'I know *enthusiasm* is despised in London, but how can I not be happy when I have found my dearest cousin again?'

'There is something you will have to be told, my dear,' said Lady Lacey. 'Sit down, Miss St George, and let me offer you a small glass of Madeira wine. I am afraid this will come as something of a shock . . .'

Clara was standing at the open door with a startled expression on her face, and from the well beyond the landing rose sounds much louder than was usual in that elegant home. Squawks, screams, men's voices, several loud thuds and a torrent of unintelligible abuses in a firm female voice.

'Laura,' said Clara in daunted tones, 'there's a black woman—and a parrot!'

Marianne crossed to the door in a wide streak of colour, leaned over the bannisters and shouted instructions. A high wail of very garbled English came back to her, and she gave one brief, pithy sentence in reply. Then she returned.

'Forgive me,' she said to Alice demurely. 'My maid has been very upset by the sea voyage, but she will settle quickly. Do not fear that I shall allow her to upset your beautiful house. You were saying, ma'am?' She turned to Lady Lacey, all politeness.

'There have been changes since you last heard from England,' Laura told her. 'This is *not* Alice's house any more. Alice owns nothing now.'

'Indeed?' Marianne's sharp dark eyes darted from

Alice to Lady Lacey. Alice sat down, quite still, and Marianne immediately came and sat beside her.

'I do not understand,' said the heiress from St Kitts.

'You must prepare yourself for a distressing shock, my dear,' said Laura. 'And one which I would spare you if I could. Alice's mother, Miss Lestrange . . .'

'You mean my dearest aunt, Lady Lacey of Holt Lacey in Wiltshire,' said Marianne promptly. 'That is, she was my cousin, not my aunt. Her mama and my grandmama were sisters, but I always called her aunt.'

'Yes—well—your cousin, my dear, was a—er—much-deceived woman,' began Laura again.

'My cousin was a lady of the utmost grace and piety,' said Marianne simply. 'Her family remained true to the Catholic faith when our ancestors left Martinique before the Revolution and fled to the British Islands. She was a model of the devout old ways. At the news of her death I wept for a week, and my papa permitted me to pay for candles to be lit for her soul in the Chapel of Sainte Monique de la Rivière. As a protestant, I do not myself believe in prayers for the departed,' confided Miss St George, 'but I knew that it would have given my dearest aunt great pleasure.'

'No doubt,' said Laura, stunned. 'Nevertheless,' she rallied, 'it appears that your—er—cousin, although in other respects a most christian lady, was not married to Sir Walter Lacey, and Alice is therefore—er—not his child in law.'

It had moved Alice beyond words to hear her mother praised, and now she sat in stony self-control, waiting for her energetic cousin to spring away from her side. She waited in vain.

'I do not believe it,' said Miss St George flatly, and a small hand went out and grasped Alice's in a tight grip.

'My dear!' cried Laura with a nervous laugh. 'Consider what you are saying! Do not think this accusation was made without the closest examination of the facts.'

'I do not care,' replied the heiress. 'My Aunt Amelie was a saint. A wise, discreet, unselfish lady of the most delicate and strict moral behaviour. It is . . . impossible to consider,' said Miss St George defiantly.

'I must ask Sir Geoffrey to confirm what I have told you.' Laura tightened her lips. 'But I can assure you . . .'

'No.'

For some moments there was silence in the room.

'Well—I will show you to your bedchamber,' Laura said finally with a small, formal smile. 'No doubt you are very tired after so long a journey. Luncheon will be served in half an hour. Will you feel well enough to join us?'

'Will Alice be there?' demanded Marianne.

'Alice normally takes luncheon upstairs.'

'Then I too will take luncheon upstairs,' replied Miss St George immediately.

Laura frowned. She had asked Percy Brown to drop in casually at lunch time, and she disliked having her plans disarranged. 'Alice may lunch downstairs today,' she said at last.

'Good,' said Miss St George. 'And now, Lady Lacey, as you so kindly suggested, perhaps Alice may show me to my room?'

'Very well.' Laura's ideas were undergoing a rapid revision. This tender shoot from the tropics was not going to be as easy to train as she had planned.

'So what is all this?' cried Marianne, whirling upon her cousin as soon as the bedroom door had closed behind them. (It was Alice's former bedroom, and Laura had lavished new rose-sprigged curtains upon it in every place that would take them—the windows, the bed, the dressing-table and round the legs of the washstand.) 'Why have you allowed that dreadful woman to supercede you, Alice, and treat you so shamefully? What of dear Holt Lacey? Has she snatched that from you too?'

'Everything,' Alice admitted. 'The property, the funds, my jewelry, even my horse. Oh Marianne, it has been terrible! But she is doing no more than she has a right to,' honesty made Alice add. 'If my papa and mama were not married, then everything I possessed does belong to Geoffrey.'

'Buncombe!' cried Marianne. 'Anyone who knew Aunt Amelie would treat that idea as laughable. They are cheating you, Alice. Telling lies to get hold of all your things.'

'No!' cried Alice in distress. 'Please do not think that, Marianne. Geoffrey may be a —a—little unkind, but he is completely honourable. He thinks very highly of his duty.'

'Dull as a day in the rainy season,' agreed her cousin, nodding. 'I remember Sir Geoffrey well. He stopped the stable boy from taking me fishing.'

'Marianne! Consorting with a village lad!'

'What else was there to do when you and my aunt were busy about the estate? I made Geoffrey promise he would not tell. He threw a fit of black temper and then —you are right—he behaved with honour. But that wife of his is not honourable at all. A poor white, if I ever saw one,' and Marianne spat contemptuously.

'Marianne!' cried Alice, laughing and shocked. 'For goodness sake! You cannot bring these savage manners to London.'

'Do you think I behave like this in a drawing-room?' asked her cousin, equally shocked. 'My dear Alice, I would have you know that my Great-Aunt Euphemie has had me most carefully brought up. But tell me,' she dragged her cousin beside her on to the edge of the bed, 'what has happened to cause this disaster? Even if it were true, they shall not bully you while I am here.'

'It is true,' sighed Alice. She gave her cousin a brief account of her situation, and then took out a letter from the pocket at her waist. 'But it is also true that Geoffrey has not behaved well. Listen to this. I asked Mr Vale, a former friend of mine,' she blushed, 'to make some legal enquiries on my behalf. He has written to me.' Alice

59

blushed again. 'Do not think that I would normally engage in correspondence with a gentleman, Marianne, but I had no-one in the world to turn to.'

'I would let nothing stop me from getting my rights,' Marianne assured her, 'not if it meant riding like Lady Godiva through the streets of Basseterre.'

'Well, I will read you Mr Vale's letter—

"Dear Miss Alice,
Mr Sellop is taking up the question of your right to the Nevis plantation. Unfortunately his notion of speed is that of a snail. He refuses to discuss the matter of your father's will, however, being the Lacey family lawyer, and your brother now being the head of the family. However, I have taken other advice, and it appears that you are correct in assuming that your father's intent has weight in the execution of his will."

'Do you understand what he means, Marianne?'
'Not precisely, but you can explain it later. Go on.'

"Had you had a father or a loving brother to protect you at the time, it is possible that Sir Geoffrey Lacey could not have behaved as he did. He is now in possession, however, and I am told that it may be up to you to sue him in the courts for a restitution of your inheritance. I will continue to explore the matter and remain, my dear Miss Alice, your cordial friend, Matthew Vale."

'How can I possibly sue Geoffrey in the courts?' asked Alice. 'He has forbidden me to see Mr Sellop. I have no money. I do not know how to find an attorney of my own, and if I did, I should not be allowed to approach him.'

'But I should have no scruples in suing Geoffrey on your behalf,' said Marianne. 'I take back my former opinion of Geoffrey. He is not honourable at all. There is something distinctly shady about all this.'

'I must say this has shaken my esteem for him,' confessed Alice. 'But that makes no difference to my problem. Even if I hated him, I should be unable to proceed any further.'

'We shall find an attorney and we shall set the proceedings going, and I shall watch with great pleasure when you throw that horrible woman out of this nice house.'

'I have not made myself clear. Geoffrey has forbidden me to consult an attorney again.'

'And does that stop you?'

'Of course.'

'My Great-Aunt Euphemie forbade me to visit the boiling-houses, but I have been there, day after day, every harvest for the last three years.'

'What for?' asked Alice.

'Why, to count the barrels of sugar coming out of the drying room, of course. Since grandpapa became ill, there has been no proper supervision. The factor is weak—his interest is not involved. Who would have inspected the crop, and collected the money for wages and made sure that the wagons were in good repair if I had not undertaken it? Fortunately Aunt Euphemie spends so much time in the chapel nowadays that it is easy to pull the wool over her eyes.'

Alice stared at her little cousin. Marianne presented a picture of delicious incompetence. Her plum-coloured travelling dress, demurely high at the neck and simply cut for ease of movement, had wide sleeves which opened to show a frothing mass of white lace that fell over the most delicate hands imaginable. The simple bodice was clipped to a tiny waist and the skirts billowed out into a width that emphasized the figure's fragility. Each time she moved, white lace matching that at her wrists peered out beneath the hem of her dress— an effect entirely acceptable, but only a hairsbreadth away from being *fast*.

'I had no idea that you were acquainted with business,' Alice said. It was hard to believe this seemingly fragile creature was running a plantation. 'Did Mr

St George's illness leave you completely without aid? Poor Marianne!'

'My grandpapa's illness,' replied the heiress frankly, 'came out of a bottle. And he did not have the grace to drink himself to death on French wines. It is my belief, Alice, that Aunt Euphemie's religious diatribes drove him to drink as a consolation, but nevertheless, he should never have allowed himself to become addicted to such common a spirit as rum.'

'Marianne! How you must have suffered!'

'Yes. Well. It is all over now, my dearest Alice, and I have made this voyage to London which I have been anxious to do for years. But you will oblige me by forgetting that grandpapa died so recently. I wore the deepest mourning until I was on the ship, but if I have to continue with it here, it will go very hard with me.'

'Where did you get such a beautiful dress?' asked Alice.

'Do you like it? Good. Aunt Euphemie ordered all my clothes from Paris, through her relations there— fortunately before grandpapa's death. She had forgotten, what with his illness and then the funeral, so when they arrived, I instructed the shipping clerk to leave them in the warehouse at the wharf and then load them aboard as soon as I knew which ship I was to travel on.'

'Of course I shall respect your wishes,' said Alice, 'and indeed with such a grandfather it would seem that mourning might be a mockery. But I cannot stop other people talking—packets arrive from the West Indies every day. People are bound to hear that you are used to going about the plantation affairs like a gentleman.'

'I can assure you that everything is conducted with the greatest propriety.' Marianne drew herself up to the top of her tiny height. 'I never see the factor or the agent without the presence of my steward and at least one respectable coloured female. And wherever my carriage goes, even on plantation roads, I take two outriders in livery. People do not "talk" about me on St

62

Kitts at all. Great-Aunt Euphemie, I would have you know Alice, is devoted to respectability. Her constant cry is *L'honneur de la famille*—she still speaks a lot of French, you understand.

'And what a relief it is to be free of it all for a while!' cried Marianne, springing from the bed and whirling round so that her little bronze boots were quite exposed. 'How many weeks are left of the Season, Alice? I propose to devote myself to London festivity. What an enjoyable time we shall have!'

'Parliament sits till some time in July,' Alice told her. 'Which will keep Sir Geoffrey in London, though some families will have left for the country by then.'

'Time enough!' she cried. 'First I must buy a crinoline exactly like the one you are wearing, dearest Alice, for these French hoops are brittle and already I am in danger of being skewered. Then I must see the bankers to whom I have been recommended and draw some bills. Then, Alice, I wish to attend a drawing-room—just to say I have been there, you know, for I am sure it will be deadly dull. Can your sister-in-law sponsor me? If not, I must rapidly make friends with a peeress. Who shall it be? I rely utterly on your guidance—and, tell me, has the Court come out of black? Not even the Queen can mourn a husband for ever . . . Then I wish to see something of the delightful countryside, which I remember as pure heaven. Those delicious evenings, with the long windows wide open and not a single bothersome mosquito! But Holt Lacey will be out for this summer, alas. Lady Lacey is the type to keep her windows tightly closed. Is it not the fashion to go to Scotland— For shooting? What do they shoot? Which of your friends has a castle Alice? There is something about the sound of a castle which arouses intense interest.'

These whirlwind plans left Alice breathless. 'You cannot know London society if you expect to move about exactly as you wish,' she said with a smile.

'And you cannot know *me* if you expect me to be stuck at home while all England is lying at the doorstep,' came the prompt reply.

CHAPTER FIVE

At the lunch table Laura's eyes, when they lit on Miss St George, were not quite so cordial as they had been at first meeting. As soon as young Mr Percy Brown came into the room, however, his eyes changed from polite interest to astounded delight and then to profound admiration within thirty seconds of falling on the heiress. In such a staid young man the effect was electric, and Alice recognized at once that any tender feelings Laura had attributed to Percy on her own behalf were pure imagination. The young man coloured, started sentences and left them dangling, pressed cold chicken pie upon Marianne with assiduous attention, and then followed the ladies from the dining-room as if he never wanted to return to his own chambers in Old Street, Lincoln's Inn, again.

Marianne behaved perfectly. After the first polite lifting of her face and rapid, shy blink of curling eyelashes on introduction, she never gave Mr Brown more than the least sideways glance or the meerest peep of her shining dark eyes from under demure lids, and a soft 'yes' or 'no' were all the words he could at first get out of her, no matter how hard he tried.

Laura settled herself comfortably and surveyed her brother's efforts with great pleasure.

'You are invited to the Brentford's ball are you not, Percy?' she asked.

'Yes, of course. Shall I have the pleasure of seeing you there, Miss St George?'

'Yes, you will,' Laura told him. 'I am sending a note to Mrs Brentford to request permission to bring our guest with me, and there is no question but that she will agree.'

'Then, may I, Miss St George—that is, if you will do

65

me the honour—er, will you? I mean, allow me to ask the favour of standing up with you for the first two dances.'

'Do you waltz, Marianne?' asked Clara curiously.

'A little,' said the heiress with modest deprecation.

'Then, if I may, Miss St George, *please* . . .' begged Percy Brown, coming as close to her in his eagerness as her skirts allowed.

'I am quite unused to London society,' Marianne hedged, 'but if Alice will stand beside me and tell me what is proper . . .'

'Alice will not be going to the ball,' said Laura.

'Then forgive me,' the girl hung her head, 'but I shall not go to the ball either.'

'You cannot mean this!' cried Percy.

Laura stared, and her mouth dropped.

'Indeed,' Marianne gave him a deeply languishing look. 'You may find me stupidly proper, Mr Brown, but I promised my Great-Aunt Euphemie never, *never* to go into company without the presence of my cousin. To do so on St Kitts, I assure you Lady Lacey, would be to lose one's good name for ever.'

Alice studied the mourning ring she wore for her father and tried to keep her face straight. She suspected that Marianne's notions of propriety were a great deal laxer than Lady Lacey's own. Meanwhile, Laura was faced with a problem. If she refused to take Alice to parties, she would lose the chance of presenting the heiress, who looked likely to become one of the sensations of the Season. And though she preferred to keep Alice firmly in the background, it was being hinted that she and Sir Geoffrey were hounding the girl beyond her deserts. Besides, thought Laura, the introduction of Miss St George into London society opened prospects of lavish entertainment at home, which her husband could hardly find fault with . . .

After a little while spent in attempts to make the heiress change her mind, Lady Lacey gave in graciously.

66

Her brother was falling in with her plans with such eagerness that it would be a pity to thwart him in any way. And what a triumph when he became the owner of Beauregarde and all its cane fields! Percy was beseeching her to change her mind. And look how sensibly the dear boy had behaved before in not losing his heart to Alice. They had escaped a very unfortunate tangle there.

'Very well,' said Laura Lacey at last. 'I will ask Mrs Brentford if I may bring Alice as well as Marianne.'

A footman brought in a salver on which was a large envelope. Lady Lacey took it while Percy Brown was talking to Marianne. 'I do not understand,' Laura said, examining a crested letter covered in purple writing. '"Sir Berkely Hawke presents his compliments to Lady Lacey . . ." Who is Sir Berkely Hawke?'

'He is Her Majesty's Governor of the Leeward Islands,' said Marianne, to everyone's surprise.

'But he asks that I shall receive his son. What is his son to me?' asked Laura, frowning.

'I believe Mr Hawke is travelling in England at the moment and—er—feels it would be polite to pay his respects to the family,' said the girl, eyes cast down. 'He knew my grandpapa and his father is a devoted friend of my Great-Aunt Euphemie. No doubt she told him to make himself known to Alice.'

'The young gentleman asked if he might be admitted,' the footman said, and on Laura's giving permission, a very smart youth with a tanned face and elegant necktie, dressed in a dark-blue coat and narrow fawn trousers of the very latest cut, was shown into the room.

He introduced himself to Lady Lacey with great aplomb, bowed to Clara, nodded to Percy and went straight across the room to Marianne.

'Well, you beat me by a day, but it was all due to winds in the Irish Sea, Miss St George,' he said, leaning over her hand. 'But for that, I would have been here on Thursday.'

'Allow me to present my dearest cousin, Miss Alice.'
Marianne retrieved her fingers.

'Your servant, ma'am,' he said.

'I take it that you have just arrived from the West
Indies?' asked Percy Brown, standing very straight.

'Yes. I came by way of Bristol, in one of the sugar
ships,' Mr Hawke told him, 'and up from there by train.
By the rights of it, I should have won by the best part
of a week as Miss St George chose the London boat.'

'Do I understand,' asked Laura with her eyebrows
raised, 'that you and Miss St George were . . . making a
race of it?'

The young man gave a bellow of laughter, and then
his sense of decorum began to take charge over a very
obvious delight in seeing the heiress again. Marianne
was sitting very demurely with no encouragement on
her small pale face.

'Not at all, ma'am,' he said hastily. 'The fact is, my
father's business made it necessary that I should be in
England at this time—to carry confidential letters and
see to his place in Berkshire and various things. And in
the islands, you know, the speed of the packets is a subject of over-riding interest.' And he gave the whole room
the benefit of a wide, ingenuous smile.

'I think it unfortunate,' said Percy Brown, 'that a
young lady's delicate constitution should be exposed to
the rigours of a sea passage at all, without making a jest
of it.'

Mr Hawke bent once more over Miss St George and
would have engaged her attention, had the girl not
turned very slightly in the direction of Percy Brown so
that Mr Hawke was summoned to Laura's side to talk
about what he intended to do in London. It appeared
that he had a wide and respectable acquaintance, and
Lady Lacey was soon satisfied enough to draw Clara
into the conversation and then let the two young people
chat with each other.

The Brown family was not well established. Sir

68

Alexander Brown had been Chancellor of the Exchequer at the time when young Geoffrey Lacey had first entered Parliament, and chance had brought the serious young Member to the attention of the great man. He had been invited to his house, been attracted to the pale charms of the elder daughter, and had believed, like the rest of the world, that Sir Alexander Brown was a wealthy man. But such was not the case. The Chancellor had shown more skill in handling the country's finances than his own, which he always imagined to be about to take a turn for the better. Ten thousand pounds were tied in with Laura's marriage settlements, and Sir Alexander had no doubt that he would accrue an equal sum by the time Clara was old enough to marry, as well as accumulate sufficient funds to provide a comfortable allowance for his only son Percy. He died in office, still a youngish man, and when his affairs were settled, Percy was left with a meagre income of some four hundred pounds a year and Clara received no portion at all.

Whilst feeling no necessity to help her brother and sister financially from her own generous settlements—even if she could—Laura did have sufficient small feelings of compunction to make her forward their interests in every possible way. Of Clara's future she felt no fear. Her sister was of the same cold disposition as herself and, allowing for a little juvenile pettishness, could be relied upon to bestow her heart in the best market available. With a little luck, Laura hoped to have her respectably settled in a year or two.

But Percy was at times a source of worry to Laura. Without showing one failing that she could pick upon and nag out of him, he sometimes displayed a distressing wish to follow his own inclinations—as in the case of Alice, whom he had treated as a lovely older sister and nothing more. The fact that Laura was at this moment thankful for his behaviour did not prevent her from wishing he was more ready to obey her careful hints.

69

But now his way seemed open to acquire that very necessary affluence. Laura began to wonder whether she had been over-hasty in presenting the heiress to society? Perhaps that refusal to go anywhere without her cousin should have been taken at its word? But no—half the Season had already gone, and at the end of it, when the House of Commons rose, Miss St George would naturally accompany the family to Holt Lacey, where Percy could also be asked to stay and the business nicely settled.

And in the meantime, young gentlemen like this Mr Hawke, whose fathers had places in Berkshire, were just the sort of company Laura would have chosen for Clara.

A burst of laughter brought her back to the present. All the others were over by the sofa now, and Mr Hawke seemed to be answering a disparaging remark from Percy Brown.

'But of course we have race meetings in the Colonies,' he was crying. 'My father has a string of horses that would not disgrace Newmarket. And the wagers run as high—is that not so, Miss St George?'

'I fancy Miss St George will know better than to think of going to Newmarket,' put in Laura with her sweet, reproving smile.

The footman came in. 'Captain Harley,' he announced, and a tall, mahogany-faced officer of upstanding figure followed him into the room.

'Forgive me for intruding on you without proper introduction, Lady Lacey,' he said with a very respectful bow, 'but the *Duke of Monmouth* will be loaded up to catch the evening tide and it was necessary that I came to see Miss St George without delay.'

'The *Duke of Monmouth*?' asked the bewildered Laura.

'My ship, Lady Lacey. We shall sail for St Kitts within eight hours, and no doubt Miss St George will wish to send letters to her relatives—Ah, my dear,' he crossed to the sofa, and his burly form forced Percy and the interested Mr Hawke to stand back. 'I trust you are completely recovered from your ordeal?'

'Ordeal?' repeated Laura faintly. Her drawing-room seemed to be slipping out of her control.

'A strong gust in the Channel, ma'am,' said the stalwart seaman. 'The young lady would have been blown overboard had one of my officers not saved her.'

'Indeed!'

'A brave fellow, Lady Lacey. Most fortunate that he should have been passing. Not that he should have been on the bridge at the time, but chance brought him to Miss St George's side just in her hour of need.'

'What a blessing,' said Laura, gazing open-mouthed at Marianne. The girl's head had wilted on her slender neck at the painful memory, and she did look as though a puff of wind might blow her fragile form across the room.

'When I rushed out from my cabin, on hearing her scream, the noble fellow had her clasped to his chest, barely supporting her strength,' went on Captain Harley. 'He intends to call this evening to make sure that Miss St George has taken no lasting harm. I am sure that you will not turn him from your door, ma'am?'

'Oh no indeed,' said Laura, wide-eyed.

'We must write to Aunt Euphemie immediately, Alice,' said Marianne, when the two girls had retired to change for dinner. 'Your mother's plantation has been in the hands of factors for so long that there may be no-one there who remembers your parents' wedding. But Aunt Euphemie must know all about it . . . that is . . .' she frowned. 'It is very strange,' she said slowly.

'What is strange?'

'Aunt Euphemie always blamed your mother for getting married so quietly. "A hole-in-the-corner affair with none of the family present," she says when she speaks of it.'

71

'Oh Marianne! That does sound as if a wedding never did take place.'

They looked at each other in doubt.

'My Aunt Amelie would never commit such a sin,' said Marianne, rallying first.

Alice fetched up a deep sigh. She crossed to her former dressing-table, where she had hung up her mother's relics before being turned out of the room. 'And yet . . .' she said sadly.

'What?'

'This was my mama's favourite portrait,' Alice told her, fingering an oval gold frame.

'What a hideous hat!' cried Marianne, coming to look. 'Like a pineapple on a bread board. And what a dreadfully old-fashioned way to wear a shawl, all hunched up round the neck. Who is she, Alice? She looks as though she rouged.'

'It is a Mrs Fitzherbert,' said Alice. 'A lady of very doubtful propriety. I could never understand why my mother held her picture in such affection, except, perhaps that she was a Catholic lady too. But even then, it was surprising. Mrs Fitzherbert, Marianne, was the—er —*chère amie* of the last King George.'

'Oh, *that* Mrs Fitzherbert!' Marianne immediately understood. 'You mean the Prince Regent's mistress? She had dozens of children by him, did she not?'

'I do not know precisely,' Alice confessed, 'but we shouldn't be talking about it, Marianne. It isn't fit.'

'You sound exactly like Great-Aunt Euphemie,' said the other girl without rancour, 'but I remember papa talking about it. He thought it all a great joke. When he was a boy, they used to wait on the wharf to catch the latest Royal scandals coming over from England, and they laid wagers on which of the old dukes would be the first to produce an heir.'

'My mother did not think Mrs Fitzherbert was loose-living,' said Alice, 'so much as wronged. A lot of people believed that a marriage had taken place between the

Prince and Mrs Fitzherbert—a secret Catholic marriage that the law would not allow to be revealed.'

'Alice!' cried Marianne, much struck. 'Suppose your parents' marriage was a secret Catholic one—how could we get proof that it took place?'

'My mother would have insisted on a Catholic marriage,' Alice replied. 'But I do not know why it should be secret.'

'Secret or not—it would not be in a Parish Church register, would it?'

'I do not know.'

'Just think—all this time those attorneys have been searching in the wrong place!'

'Do you really believe that's possible Marianne?'

'I think it's obvious. Where's my writing-desk? I must send a letter to Aunt Euphemie at once. And whom can we ask for advice on this point in England?'

CHAPTER SIX

Mrs Brentford had a large house, a hospitable nature, two nieces and the comfortable knowledge that her husband's huge income derived from trade in the north of England was no bar to their entrance into the highest society as it would have been two generations before, when the Georges occupied the throne. Reform was in the air—reform of Parliament—reform of the Church—reform of the Law—reform of the Army—reform of hospitals, charities, poorhouses and even the House of Lords. And under the exciting froth of reform, the steady tide of industrial prosperity had lifted up new faces to join the class that had ruled England for hundreds of years. Mr Brentford, son of an illiterate ironmaster, represented his county in Parliament, where he was quite content to drowse on the back benches and serve on an occasional committee without looking for higher office, so they were very generally popular.

She gave a kind welcome to Marianne and a warm one to Alice. 'I was delighted to hear that you were coming, my dear,' she said, pressing the latter's hand, 'and I trust you will call frequently. You would be a good influence on Eleanor and Lettice—where are those girls? You will find them on the dance floor I dare say.'

This was all very well, but Alice had an uncomfortable feeling that she was destined to pass the evening on a chair against the wall, among the chaperones and dowagers. She was used to being in great demand, and it was not going to be pleasant seeing her old partners leave her alone.

Then there was the vexed question of dress . . . Alice had put on a dark, high-necked gown which she felt suitable for her position, but Marianne had sent her back upstairs to change it and finally had climbed up to the top floor herself, causing great peril to her French hoops on the narrow stairs.

'This, *this* is the one you must wear,' she cried, pulling out a cerise voile.

'My dear Marianne! I had it made for a charity ball when we were supposed to go as summer flowers.'

'So wear it again tonight.'

'I never want to wear it again. It is a vulgar colour.'

'Very well. Then what of this?' said Marianne, lifting up a blue silk, its bodice and upper skirt covered with Honiton lace. 'This is simply delightful.'

'It is too grand. I should feel a fraud.'

'You are stupid!' cried Marianne, stamping her little foot. 'Now is the time when you must show your very best face to the world.'

'Marianne! Be reasonable!'

'I *am* being reasonable,' replied her cousin. 'Do you think I do not know what I am about? Whenever the harvest was disastrous, grandpapa immediately ordered a new carriage from England and put the servants into new livery. It is a matter of *business*, Alice. When your funds are lowest, you must keep your credit high.'

'I have no credit,' said Alice quietly.

'You should be ashamed of yourself!' Marianne rounded on her. 'Do you really believe these lies that Geoffrey is spreading about your Mama?'

'No. No, I don't.'

'Then show the world! This way you can demonstrate her innocence.'

The argument seemed a little specious to Alice, but they compromised on a plain ball dress of pink alpaca. A white lace shawl disguised the fact that Alice had no necklace round her throat, and she resolutely refused to borrow one from Marianne.

They were rather late, and found that the ingenious Mr Hawke had arrived before them, having procured himself an invitation the day before. He was waiting to pounce on their party, conduct Lady Lacey to a seat under a potted palm and try to engage Miss St George for the first two dances. These being promised already, however, he was quite happy to turn to Alice. She breathed a tiny sigh of relief.

As was to be expected, her former suitors flocked to make the acquaintance of the new heiress and a gratifying crowd collected at their part of the room. But Alice was not left long to stare at Captain Wargate's back and Charles Longford's shoulder. Mr Bunne had had further thoughts on the inscrutable ways of providence, and had come expressly to share them with her. He was waiting between dances to expound his theme.

'My sister has almost withdrawn from the world, Miss Alice, to devote herself to the spiritual needs of the native of the Papuan Islands and has, I am thankful to say, been largely instrumental in obtaining several thousand tracts on the Advantages of Sabbath Day Observance for their use.'

'I hope they appreciate her kind services, sir.'

'No doubt they will in time. She is working hard at the moment, gathering together a quantity of warm clothing and bound volumes of sermons and some kitchen equipment of a simple nature adapted to their use.'

Alice expressed polite interest and escaped to dance with Percy Brown.

'I have taken the liberty, my dear Miss Alice,' continued Mr Bunne when next he found her free, 'of explaining to my sister your present circumstances, and she has said that if you would care to help her in her noble work, she would welcome your assistance as an amanuensis. The remuneration would be small, as it must be when it is for charity, but you would have the satisfaction of doing good to those less fortunate than ourselves.'

Alice's second escape, this time on the arm of Mr Brentford, did not prevent her from thanking Mr Bunne quite sincerely. There was a practical element in

77

his offer of assistance which showed a true spirit of kindness.

No further chance of talk with him occurred, because to the girl's astonishment, her old suitors came back to her side one by one before each dance, and once more she was in the delightful situation of being engaged for every dance.

When Lord Locke presented himself, her surprise knew no bounds, and she could only be thankful that she was not being asked to waltz, as the young peer always contrived to trample his partner's feet. She held no ill-will towards Lord Locke, appreciating his need to get some help in raising his noisy crowd of brethren, and faced him good humouredly across the line, quite grateful that he had decided not to let their acquaintance drop.

'Your cousin seems quite undaunted by London,' remarked Lord Locke, when the figure brought them together.

'Yes, indeed.'

'Although the society in the Colonies must be more restricted.'

'I believe so.'

'Perhaps the lives of young ladies in those regions are less sheltered than those over here?' hazarded her partner.

Alice immediately understood. Marianne's instant popularity had made Lord Locke wonder whether his new intended might have a touch of immodesty in her behaviour. So she expounded, each time the dance brought them together again, on the extraordinarily protected lives which young ladies on St Kitts were forced to lead and upon the very great religious bent of Great-Aunt Euphemie.

His Lordship was obviously relieved. To be frank, he could not afford to be fussy, but shrank from inviting a flirt to share the honours of Locke Place.

'And nothing can exceed your cousin's devotion to

yourself, Miss Alice,' he told her in gratitude. 'Indeed it is elevating to find a young lady so dearly attached to her friend.'

These words raised an unpleasant suspicion in Alice's mind. Was it *possible* . . .? She looked across at Marianne when she was returned to Lady Lacey's side, but the girl was hiding her face behind her fan in response to a remark from one of her many squires. Alice frowned. She remembered all those definite little statements—'I will only go if Alice goes too'—and wondered whether the heiress could be prefacing her acceptance of partners with something like—'Only if you ask my cousin'. Alice blushed angrily.

'May I engage you for the next dance before I lose the chance yet again?' Someone was bending over her. It was Matthew Vale. No-one looked better in a ball-room; the black evening coats that had stayed in fashion since the fifties set off his wide shoulders admirably, and his height made him an outstanding figure in any room. Nevertheless, Alice gave him a chilly glance.

'Only if—' she began impetuously.

'Only if what?' he asked, intrigued.

'Only if you are not forced to do so by Marianne,' Alice had been going to say, but she had stopped herself in time.

'Do tell me,' said Mr Vale.

'It was nothing,' said Alice stiffly. 'Have you been introduced to my cousin, Miss St George?'

'Not yet. I was hoping that you might perform that service later. At the moment she seems very fully occupied.'

Alice's momentary pique subsided. 'Oh Mr Vale,' she cried, raising contrite eyes to his. 'It was so very kind of you to seek out Mr Sellop and then write to me. I am deeply obliged.'

'I wish I could do more,' he responded, leading her on to the floor.

79

'It seems,' Alice told him, 'that Betty-Lou's word is not to be trusted. There was a great rowdy confrontation this morning between her and Phoebe, who is Marianne's black maid. Phoebe knew Betty-Lou when she was banished to St Kitts for some misdemeanour, and she tackled her when they met on the staircase and accused her of telling a pack of lies.'

'You mean,' said Matthew Vale very seriously, and his arm tightened about Alice's waist, 'that all this unpleasant business will blow over and things will be exactly as they were before.'

'No,' said Alice sadly. 'Betty-Lou screamed and cursed, and the whole house was in an uproar—I have never seen Geoffrey so displeased. But Phoebe could not shake her word that my mother had never been married. She stuck to that. It seems untrue to say, however, that she was my grandfather's child. She is known to be the daughter of a sailor on a trading schooner.'

'So there is no improvement in your outlook,' said Matthew Vale. 'I am sorry.' But he did not, she noticed, hold her the less close.

'Well, it does mean that I own Frenchman's Point Plantation,' said Alice, 'and I have a home of my own to go to, however poor and small. For stay with Laura after Marianne departs I cannot do.'

There was a long pause in conversation until the dance concluded. Had an anxious mama been watching Mr Vale's behaviour, she would have been delighted by the settled gloom that hung over his face.

'It is very far away, Miss Alice,' he said at last. 'Your sugar plantation. Your friends would be very sad to see you go.'

'Perhaps I had better return to my seat now, Mr Vale,' said Alice, gently extracting herself from his grip. 'The music stopped several minutes ago.'

'So who is this Mr Matthew Vale?' Marianne demanded,

80

when the two cousins were sipping hot chocolate in Marianne's room after the ball.

'He is . . . a gentleman,' Alice repressively replied.

'That much is obvious, and also he is a very accomplished dancer and one with a good sense of dress, and if he had just landed from a ship and I were asked to judge without knowing, I should say he was very much a man of the world,' said the heiress. 'But what is he to you?'

'A—a—a—dancing partner, that is all.'

'Don't talk claptrap! Is he not the man who wrote to you about your father's will? A dancing partner! And let me tell you, Alice, no other partner brought that certain look into your face tonight.'

'Is it true?' asked Alice aghast. 'Did I show the world?'

'No of course not, you silly. Nothing to raise a whisper. But I am very observant in these matters. It is my French blood,' said Marianne with pride, 'and I know you have a tenderness for him. Why does he not come forward and offer for you now, when you so badly need a protector? He seems to have money, and he is certainly old enough to know his own mind.'

'He is most unfortunately placed,' sighed Alice, 'and could not offer for me if he wished to.'

'Do not tell me he is not independent. He has the manner of a gentleman of large means.'

'Mr Vale,' Alice explained, 'is the nephew and heir of the Duke of Severn. Have you ever heard of the Duke of Severn, Marianne?'

'Ooooooh—who has not? So you have thoughts of being a rich duchess, Alice?'

'No, indeed. You see, Marianne, Mr Vale is completely dependent on His Grace's goodwill. He gets a handsome allowance and is allowed to use the Severn homes, I believe. But should he behave—should he marry—against the duke's wishes, His Grace would withdraw his favour and Mr Vale would have nothing at all.'

'He would still inherit the dukedom when his uncle dies,' pointed out Marianne.

'Perhaps. Though if the old man were angry enough, he might marry himself and produce his own heir.'

'I thought he was about ninety! Well—anyway, he was the same vintage as grandpapa, and how grandpapa loved to hear about him! Wine, wickedness and women —my grandfather revelled in the tales. "Just like the good old days before all this namby-pamby soberness!" he used to say. But I expect he only did it to annoy Great-Aunt Euphemie.'

'The duke is not *quite* as bad as that, I think,' said Alice. 'At any rate, he confines his—er—excesses to the continent. When he visits England he is still received in all the best homes.'

'And does Mr Vale take after his uncle?'

Alice hesitated. 'I should be wrong to conceal from you that there have been stories . . .' she began, and indeed there had. Even a young lady's ears could not be protected from all the tales of the wild set with whom Matthew Vale associated from time to time. And yet— Alice thought about what she *knew* as opposed to what people *said*. Mr Vale was an impeccable dancing partner, an agreeable neighbour to have beside one at the dinner table and a very useful squire in time of trouble —was he not the only man to find an umbrella at the unfortunate garden party at the Harrovale's? And had not Alice's and Laura's been the only two bonnets that were not completely ruined by the rain? 'People always exaggerate the follies of unmarried men,' Alice said firmly. 'And yet—and yet, they do say that the duke is bringing strong pressure on Mr Vale to marry.'

'And has His Grace chosen the bride?'

'Oh no, no, Marianne. He is an indulgent uncle, I believe. But you do see . . .'

'See what?'

'That however indulgent the duke may be, he would never permit his heir to marry someone who—who was

82

born without a father's name to call her own,' and Alice broke down and cried bitterly.

Marianne provided immediate warm comfort, a clean handkerchief and a small towel to keep the tears off the pink alpaca.

'We were born too late,' she said sympathetically. 'Forty years ago Mr Vale would have picked you up and thrown you over the saddle of his horse and ridden straight off with you to Gretna Green.'

At which unlikely picture both girls were overcome with giggles.

'Phoebe will call you tomorrow at an early hour,' Marianne told Alice before she left for her own room. 'I have arranged for Mr Sellop to call and see us early, before Lady Lacey is likely to be down.'

'Arranged for Mr Sellop to come *here*? My dear Marianne, how could you possibly have arranged anything so unlikely as that at a ball?'

'I asked Mr Hawke to do it for me,' Marianne replied.

CHAPTER SEVEN

But it was not old Mr Sellop who rose to his feet shyly when Marianne and Alice, a little bleary-eyed, entered the small sitting-room on the following morning. It was Mr Christopher, the young attorney whom Alice had met before. He explained that Mr Sellop felt unable to act for Alice, and he offered his services instead.

'You are very young,' said Marianne critically. 'Are you sure you know your way about?'

The young man said, not without colouring, that Mr Sellop could vouch for his competence and had sent him as being the most useful person Miss Alice could consult, 'Because,' admitted Mr Christopher, 'my time is at your disposal, which that of more famous lawyers could not be.'

Alice had liked him from the first, and immediately began to lay before him the idea which had occurred to her and Marianne.

'My mama was a Catholic, and is not likely to have been married in a Protestant church. So all the search for records will have been in the wrong place, Mr Christopher.'

But that was not so. The young man explained that since the Act of Reform Catholic marriages were registered just as the others were, in churches or wherever the ceremony might have taken place.

'And are you sure you searched everywhere on the island?'

In each church, in each parish, at the registry office in Basseterre. He had examined records for the years 1839, 1840 and 1841, to be sure of covering the period widely. He had enquired at various Great Houses and he had spoken to many people who still remembered Miss Amelie Lestrange.

'But after all, Nevis is only a tiny place,' commented Marianne. 'To be married, she would go to St Kitts to be with her family . . .' her voice trailed off and her eyes met those of Alice. Had not Great-Aunt Euphemie herself called the marriage 'a hole-in-the-corner affair'?

'Do not imagine I did not think of that,' said Mr Christopher eagerly. 'When I drew a blank on Nevis, naturally I went across to St Kitts and carried out a full enquiry there. But the answer was the same. There was nothing—nothing to show that a marriage had taken place.'

'Wait a minute,' cried Alice. 'There is a Catholic Chapel at Gorman House, not far from Holt Lacey. My mother went to mass there regularly. Would she not have chosen to hold her wedding there, after her arrival in England?'

'Exactly the conclusion I came to myself,' said Mr Christopher. 'It was the first place I went to make enquiries on this side of the Atlantic. But the story there and everywhere is the same. Lady Lacey arrived in England and, of course, no-one expected a wedding because she had been married to Sir Walter before she left her own home.'

'It is incredible,' sighed Alice.

'It is,' said Mr Christopher, rumpling his hair. 'No-one mentions your mother without speaking of her high reputation. One cannot understand the thing at all.'

'Well at least I am the owner of her plantation,' said Alice. 'You have not heard about Betty-Lou, Mr Christopher. She has confessed that her rights to Frenchman's Point were founded on a pack of lies.'

'Oh dear,' said the young attorney.

'Are you not pleased?' asked Alice, rallying him. 'Surely if I am your client you would rather I had some means of paying your bill?'

'Oh dear,' he said again.

'What is it?' asked Marianne sharply.

'I looked into the ownership of Frenchman's Point

when Mr Vale brought up the matter,' he confessed, 'and the sad fact is, Miss Alice, that if your mother left no will, as I believe is the case, and in default of legitimate heirs, the plantation does not descend to you or Betty-Lou at all.'

'No!' cried Alice in despairing tones. It was a harder blow than she had been prepared for. At least the ownership of Frenchman's Point had given her some tiny feeling of independence, but now she was back to being a pauper again.

'Then who does it belong to?' asked Marianne.

'To some distant relations of the late Miss Lestrange who live on the island of St Kitts. Their name is St George, and the present owner is a young lady, I believe. I have the particulars here . . .'

A burst of laughter interrupted him. Alice and Marianne were highly amused.

'Have I said something stupid?' asked the attorney.

'No. Not at all. Only this is such a surprise. I apologize for not introducing you earlier—this is my cousin, Mr Christopher. Miss Marianne St George from St Kitts.'

'Well, upon my soul, what a fortunate event!'

'Make out a document,' Marianne told him peremptorily. 'Have it drawn up properly without any legal quibble at all. I give all my rights to Frenchman's Point Plantation to my cousin Alice Lacey—no, Alice Lestrange—no, you had better just put *Alice*. And do it now, today. Then at least on this one point she shall know where she stands.'

'But, Miss St George!' Mr Christopher was appalled at this off-hand treatment of property.

'But Marianne, I cannot let you do such a thing for me!'

'Do it,' said the heiress, snapping her fingers. 'And Alice, if you dare to thank me, I shall cut you dead. Do you think I could harvest your own land while you lived on charity? What about *L'honneur de la famille*? You would do exactly the same for me, you know you would. Well, Mr Christopher, can you or can you not do as I say?'

The attorney said he would be pleased to execute Miss St George's commands.

'But this has nothing to do with Sir Walter Lacey's will,' Marianne said, 'and we have heard that it did not have to be disregarded simply because Alice's name was written wrong.'

'That is true,' said Mr Christopher. 'It is a nice point, and I believe Mr Sellop allowed himself to be over-persuaded. There seem to be clear grounds of Sir Walter's intent.'

'So what should my cousin do now?'

'I shall have to take advice on the matter, but have little doubt what that would be. Miss Alice must take her brother to court and sue for the restoration of her inheritance.'

'No!' cried Alice, her hands flying to her cheeks. 'I could not drag the Lacey name through the mud like that. It would be printed in the newspapers!'

'Don't be a fool,' hissed Marianne. 'Think of all the things he has done to you. We shall proceed,' she informed Mr Christopher loftily, 'as you suggest. Please take advice, and make it the very best advice available, and while we are about it, send another man to the West Indies. I know you did everything that you were able, Mr Christopher, but I wish somebody to see my Great-Aunt Euphemie. I feel she must know more of this than she has ever said. Send a good man and send him first to me for letters of introduction. I have already written to my aunt, so she will know what it is all about.'

'No—wait!' cried Alice. 'Don't do anything, please Mr Christopher. How can I possibly pay you for this? I do not even know if I can afford your visit today. But voyages to the West Indies and court cases are very expensive. I simply do not have the means.'

Mr Christopher was heard to mumble something which included the name of Mr Vale.

'No!' cried Alice again. 'That is out of the question. There has been a mistake. Mr Vale was so kind as to take a message on my behalf . . .'

'It is not a concern of Mr Vale's. You are right, Alice,' said Marianne rising grandly. 'The bills,' she told the attorney, 'are to be sent to me.'

He bowed.

'Marianne, you cannot do this. Court cases drag on for months and months and cost thousands of pounds.'

'You may pay me back when you have received your fortune again, if you insist,' Marianne acceded. 'But in the meantime, I would do much more if it helped to clear dear Aunt Amelie's name.'

'I cannot understand why you came down so early,' said Lady Lacey, bustling into the room. 'Clara is still asleep and I myself . . .' She stopped and stared. The attorney, who had edged his way towards the door, bowed hesitantly, uncertain what to do.

'Lady Lacey, may I present Mr Christopher?' asked Marianne with great presence of mind.

'From the West Indies?' asked Laura, eyeing him. The young man's clothes were neat rather than fashionable.

'Mr Christopher is the attorney who is handling my affairs in England,' Marianne said with a warning look at Alice.

'It would be far more suitable,' Lady Lacey said bridling, 'if Sir Geoffrey's own man were to advise you. And I cannot understand what he is doing *here*. Ladies do not see men of business in their own home, Miss St George, except under extraordinary circumstances and in the presence of their fathers and brothers.' She turned to the luckless attorney. 'You cannot expect to be received in this house again unless the arrangement has been made through Sir Geoffrey Lacey,' she said.

'Mr Vale,' announced a footman, and Matthew followed him into the room. He bowed to the ladies and shot an enquiring glance at young Mr Christopher and then, to Alice's profound relief, turned his back on the attorney and allowed him to escape from the room.

'This is very kind of you,' said Laura Lacey, greeting the Duke of Severn's heir.

'I came to make sure that none of the ladies had suffered from their exertions at the ball last night,' Mr Vale said blandly.

'You are too kind. Mrs Brentford arranges these affairs with great taste, does she not? A little old-fashioned, perhaps, preferring candlelight to gas, but the effect was certainly charming.'

'But think of the work it will cause her poor servants,' said Alice. 'After a party at Holt Lacey it takes days to clean the sconces and the wax cannot be coaxed off the carpets for several weeks.'

'Practicality before romance, Miss Alice?' asked Matthew, cocking an amused eyebrow at her.

'I am afraid so,' she confessed. 'Papa preferred candles, but I had gas laid to the main rooms here as soon as the house became mine.'

'The house has never actually been yours in fact, Alice,' said Laura stiffly.

A swift riposte had sprung to Marianne's lips, but at that moment the footman threw open the door again and announced, 'Mrs Wibsley Gorman,' and a broad lady in widows weeds sailed into the room.

'Laura,' she briefly greeted Lady Lacey. 'Matthew, you here?' She recognized Mr Vale. Then, 'My dear, dear Alice,' she cried in booming tones.

'Godmama!' cried Alice and ran to embrace her.

'What is this I hear?' asked Mrs Gorman, sinking on to the sofa and taking up every inch of it with her wide black bombazine. 'Can it be true, Laura, that your husband is setting aside his father's will and casting my goddaughter into the poorhouse?'

'You must allow me to offer you refreshment,' Laura

said hastily ringing the bell. 'Did you come up by the night train, Mrs Gorman, to have arrived so early from Somerset?'

'I have not come from Somerset today,' said the older lady, who was divesting herself of various shawls. 'It has taken me some time to arrange my affairs, and then I travelled up by road, taking two nights on the way. Nothing would hinder me from coming when I heard the infamous news. I reached London last evening. Pass me my lorgnette, Alice—you will find it in my reticule. I do not believe I am acquainted with that young woman.' And she stared at Marianne so hard that the accomplished young lady drooped and looked forlorn.

'This is my cousin from St Kitts, Godmama,' Alice explained, and Marianne sank into a polite acknowledgement of the introduction.

'Only parlourmaids curtsy like that nowadays, my dear,' said Mrs Wibsley Gorman. 'A bob is quite sufficient except, of course, at Court. But you have the appearance of one who has been well brought up. St George . . . yes. Yours is the heretic branch of the family.'

Marianne's eyes sparkled, but her face stayed demure.

'We,' said Mrs Gorman, expanding her bosom, 'saw fit to remain with the old faith, as did the Lestranges, and I shall never forgive your papa, Alice, for preventing you from coming with your mama to mass.

'But this is not the point,' she continued. 'I came here, Laura Lacey, to find out why you and Geoffrey have been spreading wicked slander on the name of Alice's unfortunate mother. If what I hear is true, some very nasty work has been taking place.'

'I assure you, Mrs Gorman,' cried Laura indignantly, 'that you have no right whatsoever to use those expressions!'

'Indeed! Let me hear more. And let me assure you, Laura, that any argument you may offer me that my dearest friend Amelie Lacey passed her life in mortal

91

sin will be treated as the falsehood it is. She was a lady of impeccable breeding, which is more than can be said of Geoffrey's mother, although she brought a fortune in coals.'

'Mrs Gorman!' cried Laura, deeply offended.

'I hear that you are treating my goddaughter no better than a servant,' went on Mrs Gorman. 'Turning her out of her room and making her sleep under the leads and take her meals apart. And she the true owner of Holt Lacey without a proper man to protect her! You should be ashamed, Laura Lacey, and I shall make it my business to see that the world thinks so.'

'I fear that a true gentleman would depart at this moment, but I confess I would not miss it for all the tea in China,' said a low voice in Alice's ear. She had retreated out of the line of fire to a corner near the window and now found Mr Vale at her side.

'I have come,' went on Mrs Gorman, 'to snatch Alice from the bosom of this unworthy family and take her under my own roof until this lying persecution can be stopped at its source.'

'May heaven forgive you for those words, Mrs Gorman,' screeched Laura self-righteously. 'There has been no lie. The facts of Alice's birth are accepted by the law.'

'We shall see.'

'And we have *not* behaved unkindly to Alice,' continued Laura a trifle wildly. 'She attended the Brentford's ball last night—did you not Alice? She danced till the small hours, while Clara was often obliged to sit out. Tell her, Alice. It is wicked and cruel to say Sir Geoffrey and I are unkind!' and Laura raised a handkerchief to her eyes and dissolved into gulps of genuine misery and exasperation.

Mrs Gorman turned ponderously to Alice. 'Is this true my child?' she asked.

'It is true that I went to the Brentford's ball last night, Godmama,' Alice admitted.

'And she is *not* sleeping with the servants,' said Laura

in an angry muddle. 'She had to change her room to —to accommodate Miss St George, but she is moving down into a guest chamber tonight.'

Marianne shot a wicked glance of triumph at her cousin.

'Then perhaps I have been misinformed.' Mrs Gorman rose to her feet. 'Laura,' she said, 'I reserve judgment. Alice, you will call on me tomorrow afternoon at Lady Arthur's house where I am staying for the present. I propose to spend the morning with Violet. Matthew,' she looked Mr Vale up and down. 'You did not see fit to call upon me while you were down at Severn Abbey in February.'

'Forgive me, Mrs Gorman. I feared that my companions were not such as you would care to meet.'

She sniffed. 'It's time you settled down, young man and has been for the last ten years,' she said. 'I must speak to the duke about it when he is next in England.'

'Was Christopher helpful?' Mr Vale asked Alice in a whisper. She had only time to assure him that he had been before she went over to attend to Laura and Mr Vale departed.

CHAPTER EIGHT

'Oh Marianne, what are we to do?' asked Alice as soon as the two girls were alone together. 'Here is my godmother, determined to carry me off to the country when I do so wish to be in London. How can I communicate with Mr Christopher from all that distance? And what is to happen to you? You came to London expressly to enjoy the Season.'

'Of course we must not leave London now,' Marianne agreed.

'Perhaps it would be best, dear Marianne, if I am forced to go, for you to stay here under Laura and Geoffrey's protection. I know Laura likes to have you here because it gives her a chance to hold parties on a larger scale than she would for Clara.'

'You must remain in London, or your situation will slip from people's memories. Down in the country you would be quite forgotten, and I daresay would end up by marrying a curate. And it is right that your presence here should make Laura uncomfortable—look how she climbed down when Mrs Gorman attacked her. Is this not a very nice room?'

'Indeed I am very happy to be on this floor near you again,' said Alice thankfully. 'And to have a closet for my dresses. And to be away from Betty-Lou. She has been coming to me in the early mornings to weep and groan and beg my forgiveness, and it is a little hard to bear.'

'She should be whipped for all the trouble she has caused,' said Marianne coldly. 'But she will not vex you long. I heard Clara say she is to be sent down to Holt Lacey.'

'And what are we to do about my godmother?'

Marianne considered. 'I think you should tell Mrs

95

Gorman the exact situation,' she said. 'She is obviously a lady of some importance and Lady Lacey is frightened of her. It will give you countenance to have a friend like that at hand.'

'I don't think Laura will permit her to come to the house again.'

'Nonsense! Is not her son a close associate of Sir Geoffrey's in the party? Believe me, the Laceys would find themselves much blamed if they tried to separate you from your godmother at such a time. These things arrange themselves. Does Mrs Gorman have a London home? If we could live with her in town it would be acceptable. I must confess it would be a relief to be free of that tiresome Clara.'

'I think it most unlikely,' Alice said. 'Mrs Gorman's daughter-in-law is in hourly expectation of her confinement and everybody will wish to shield her from excitement at such a time.'

'Then if the worst comes to the worst, you and I will set up house together and hire a respectable woman to live with us and act as our duenna.'

'Marianne! What an idea! How could two young ladies live on their own in London? Set up house! I would not know where to begin.'

'Well I do. You can rent very superior apartments in Belgrave Mansions for four hundred and fifty pounds the year complete with elegant furniture. It would not be quite so distinguished as one might wish, but it would be easier to arrange than a house. The respectable woman would be a little more difficult to find, perhaps.'

'How on *earth* do you discover facts like these when you have been such a short time in England?' asked Alice, lost between disapproval and admiration.

'I asked Mr Charles Longford, and he found it all out for me,' said Marianne simply. 'He is quite a sensible man once one gets him to stop spouting poetry.'

Alice surveyed her tender-looking little cousin with

respect. She had considered herself emancipated in her detailed knowledge of the business of being an heiress, and Holt Lacey had been under her control since her mother died. She knew every inch of the estate, the names, characters and competence of all the tenants, and whilst she had been wise enough to leave entirely in Mr Sellop's hands the funds acquired when the railway lands had been sold, she had kept herself closely informed of the steady rise in value of the Bristol properties and the falling rents in residential Bath. All this she had inherited from Amelie's careful charge, for Sir Walter Lacey had shown brilliant acumen in creating opportunities for expansion, but he was quite incapable of tedious, day-by-day, regular supervision.

But although such an upbringing had brought her far more experience and capability than many a gentleman was accustomed to bring to his own affairs, Alice knew that there had always been some solid masculine figure in the background to whom she could turn in times of crisis—Sir Walter himself, and latterly Sir Geoffrey. She doubted whether she could have managed entirely on her own.

She now realized the great difficulties that would beset a young lady who saw a large plantation going to ruin under the slack hands of a drunken old man and his recluse of a sister. Marianne had had to use whatever tools came to hand. It had certainly made her quick to seize an opportunity.

'Laura finds herself unwell, and is resting in her room,' Clara told them reproachfully at lunch time. Sir Geoffrey had left his club to join them, and had reached the front steps at the same time as Percy Brown.

'I trust you did not venture out this morning, Miss St George,' Percy asked tenderly. 'The wind and the rain made it totally unfit for a lady's constitution.'

'It was all the fault of Mrs Gorman,' Clara went on.

'No. It was a great pity. I was to have had my first

ride in the park, but of course that was out of the question,' Marianne replied to her suitor.

'Is Mrs Gorman in town?' enquired Sir Geoffrey. 'I was talking to Gorman this morning, but he did not mention it. He tells me if it comes to a division, we cannot count on the Irish vote this time.'

'Do you enjoy riding in the West Indies, Miss St George?'

'She told Laura,' said Clara with malice, 'that you and she were being grossly unkind to Alice.'

'In general the climate is too hot,' Marianne informed Percy in clear, light tones, 'and I am little used to it. A gentle walk around the grounds at Beauregarde in the cool before sundown is all that my aunt normally permits me.'

Sir Geoffrey raised his head and frowned. 'What did you say, Clara?' he demanded.

'But some of my happiest memories,' continued Marianne industriously, 'are centred round the time I spent at dear Holt Lacey . . .'

'Mrs Gorman said that you and Laura were locking Alice up in a servant's room and not allowing her to eat,' reported Clara, who felt quite cheated at missing the scene.

'. . . where Sir Walter had me mounted on a dear little shaggy pony, not much bigger than a dog, so that I could accompany Alice on her rides.'

'What! Is this true? Alice, how *dare* you . . . ?'

'Do you not think, Sir Geoffrey,' asked Marianne, turning soulful eyes to his, 'that the lanes around Holt Lacey, so heavily shaded, so deep-bottomed, are not the most charming in the world?'

'What? Yes. Er . . . no doubt. Alice, who gave you leave to complain to Mrs Gorman?'

'It is a part of England that I too love very dearly,' agreed Percy, who had eyes and ears only for Miss St George.

'I merely wrote to my godmother to acquaint her of the facts, Geoffrey,' Alice said. 'Laura gave me permission at the time.'

'And those gallops across the hillside! Do you remember, Alice, how my pony baulked at that little brook and I went head over heels into the water?'

'I must see Laura about this,' said Sir Geoffrey, angrily pushing back his plate and striding from the room.

'My dear Miss St George,' cried Percy Brown, all worry and concern. 'I trust you took no harm? I wish that I had been there to protect you.'

'Perhaps you will give us your protection if we ride this afternoon?' Marianne asked demurely. 'The sun is shining brilliantly now. Shall we go riding, Alice? Do you not feel the need of fresh air, Clara?'

And her own sweet-tempered roan was brought round for Alice as naturally as if she had never ceased to own it, and her second horse was allotted to Marianne. But for Clara the groom led up Sir Geoffrey's oldest hack, which had been fitted with a side-saddle for the occasion. He was an old, trusted servant who had been with the Laceys for twenty years.

The groom shepherded the ladies out of the quiet square and along the short stretch of Oxford Street which they must traverse to reach the park. Here his services were really necessary because of the heavy traffic. The International Exhibition might have been a dismal failure (unlike its great forerunner of 1851), but London still drew crowds of foreigners each year to stare at the fashions, gape at the huge rising arches of St Pancras Station—said to be the widest in the world—or, if they were especially daring, to go down into the bowels of the earth and actually travel on the very first underground railway.

Tourists stared out from their black-lacquered hackney cabs at streets crowded with victorias, hansoms, broughams, landaus, gigs, omnibuses, peddlars' carts, brewers' drays and coal-wagons pulled by steaming

99

horses. It was almost impossible at times to pick one's way.

The fine weather after such an unpleasant morning had brought out many of their acquaintances, and Mr Brown was not called upon to protect Miss St George against the dangers of a gallop, as their progress through the park was constantly impeded by the approach of friends. Nevertheless, he clung to her side like a limpet, and word went round that the Lacey family's greed knew no bounds—grabbing two fortunes in the inside of one season.

'Well, Alice,' Mrs Gorman said when she presented herself at Lady Arthur's house the following afternoon. 'I hear you are to take Geoffrey to law about your father's will.'

'Now how on earth has that story got around?' Alice demanded.

'Is it not true then? You should, you know. If you cannot undertake it yourself, then I will ask John to help you. I know he's Geoffrey's friend, but my friendship with your mother came first, and so I shall tell him.'

'I'm not quite sure . . .' Alice began slowly, 'that my dearest mama would be cleared even if I were to win a case against my brother. I might get back my inheritance, but that would not prove that mama ever married papa.'

'A large fortune is more use in getting a husband than a clean birth record,' said Mrs Wibsley Gorman, a thoroughly practical woman. 'Though of course it is better to have both if you can. How came your mother to be so shockingly careless, Alice, as to leave her marriage unrecorded? For marriage there must have been. Whatever the lawyers may say, you know and I know, dear child, that your mama would never have attended mass so regularly had she been living in an irregular way. And Father Sturrocks agrees with me. It is not to be thought of. Why don't your relatives in the Colonies dig up some sort of evidence that would satisfy Mr Sellop? John said that perhaps your mama might even claim to be a wife at Common Law, living as she did so long as your papa's known wife—but that, of course, would not remove the shame.'

Alice explained about the petitions that had already gone off to Great-Aunt Euphemie, and also about the doubts she felt about the chance of anything coming to light over there after such an exhaustive earlier search. 'Mr Sellop did hope, ma'am, that when his assistant drew blank on that side of the ocean, he would find that mama had been married at Gorman Park.'

'Quite out of the question. I visited Amelie the very day after Walter brought her home from Bristol. Having heard so much about her, I was most curious to see her in person. And she was "my dearest wife" and "Lady Lacey" right from the start. And now that I come to think of it, Sir Walter had told me how much I would love the wife he "was bringing back from the West Indies." It never occurred to any of us but that he had married her there.'

'If only my grandpapa had allowed it, they would have been married years before,' sighed Alice, 'and none of this trouble would have arisen.'

'No, no. Walter could not have done that. He was not his own master, my dear.'

'What do you mean?'

'Your mother's fortune would have been too small for them to live on and your grandpapa—your *Lacey* grandpapa—had refused to settle Sir Walter's debts. It was a surprise to all of us he dared come back to England.'

'Do you mean he was in danger of being sent to the Marshalsea?' asked Alice, blinking at this unlikely portrait of her splendid sire. 'I always understood his youth had been spent wildly, but . . .'

'My dear, if you had seen the manor house at that time! The roof leaked in a hundred places, the garden wall was down, old Sir William was quite unable to manage, while your father scampered about the world with his creditors at his heels.'

'Was it as bad as that?'

'Gambling of course was quite respectable in those days,' Mrs Gorman remembered, 'and your father was not alone in playing high. I've heard it said that Sir Walter bet ten thousand pounds on the turn of a card one night, lost it, then tossed a coin for his horse and had to walk home halfway across the county.'

'No wonder my grandfather was distressed!'

'He was indeed, my dear. That was why Walter had to leave the country—well, perhaps it was the matter of the duel, we never learnt precisely.'

'A duel!' cried Alice in dismay.

'Oh yes. There was no form of folly at which he did not try his hand. But that's how young men were in those days. My brother was exactly the same. I remember my own father tearing out handfuls of hair in his rage.'

'Is that why papa married Geoffrey's mother then?' Alice asked. 'I could never understand why he did so when he had given his heart to my mama.'

'Oh yes, it was all for money,' said Mrs Gorman. 'When he came back to England he actually found the bailiffs in the drawing-room, so they say, and your grandfather lying ill while they waited to snatch the sheets off his very bed.'

'No!'

'Your father's debts had put such a strain on the place that it was all to be sold up.'

'Good heavens! I have never heard this before.'

'No. It is quite forgotten now. For things soon came right again. When your father saw the damage he had done and the sorrow he had caused, he set about immediately and put all thoughts of your mother aside. He was always one to repent for his bad ways, was

Walter Lacey. All flash and flare and devil-take-you, but at bottom a man of excellent heart.'

'I know,' said Alice softly.

'Well, your papa asked for Miss Stebbings, who was staying with relatives at Bristol, and her family jumped at it, for they had not thought to look so high as the Laceys before. The coal mines that Daisy brought with her saved the Lacey estates, and your father was soon adding to them, for once he settled down he proved an excellent manager. He did indeed. In ten years Holt Lacey and the farms were in excellent heart and he had begun to dabble in the railways.'

'And my mother?' asked Alice, thinking of the lonely Amelie Lestrange on the tiny island so far away, eating her heart out for the handsome rogue from England who she had expected to come back and make her his bride.

'He never forgot her,' Mrs Gorman said. 'Geoffrey was born, and Daisy lived to put her son into breeches, but when she died—and long before he should have put off mourning—your father was back off to Nevis after your mother. It is a very romantic tale.'

'Yes,' agreed Alice, 'if only it had had a happy ending.'

'We have not seen the end of it, my dear,' said her godmother bracingly, 'and in the meantime, how is Laura treating you, Alice? I understand she does not starve and beat you now as she did at first.'

'Indeed, ma'am, people have shockingly exaggerated! And things have been so much easier for me since Marianne arrived. Laura has sent Mrs Vesey away, but that was only to be expected, and Mrs Vesey has found a home with her brother, so it is not all too bad. But I do not like to see my loyal servants suffer. Mary will be the next to go—she was my maid.'

'Now let me see . . . that is Mary Scott from Holt Hurslem, ain't it? Is she as good a clear-starcher as her mother used to be?'

'Oh yes. She washes all my personal things herself.'

'Then I may be able to find a place for Mary if I stay in London,' said Mrs Gorman. 'My own maid was too old to bring up from the Park and there's no-one here to get up my frills properly. These modern gels iron them all flat like a shirt tail. But first let me hear what your plans are, my dear.'

Alice explained how things now stood in Portman Square. 'We should like to stay in London—Marianne and I—as long as we can,' she concluded, 'because of the legal affairs we shall have to attend to.'

'There will be a tremendous dust up when news of this case reaches Geoffrey!' said the old lady. 'I can hardly believe he will allow you to stay with him then.'

'Cannot such things be settled amicably, ma'am?'

'Amicably! When if you win, Geoffrey will go back to being a modest baronet with no proper place of his own but that overgrown farmhouse in Derbyshire? My dear Alice, he is likely to tear you limb from limb!'

'Well he has no right to,' declared Alice vigorously. 'He is going against the expressed wishes of our dear papa.'

'You can depend on it. Sir Walter's wishes do not hold much chance against Geoffrey's love of money.'

'I am afraid you are right, Godmama. With all their increase in income, he seems to be much worse than he was before. Positively mean,' added Alice on reflection. 'He has forbidden fires, although the evenings are so cold. And I am sure coal was never stinted in that house when I was in charge.'

'It is the way of some men, my dear. The more they get, the louder they hear the clang of the poorhouse door. When Geoffrey learns you are out to get your own back, he will explode like a volcano.'

'Then what shall I do?' asked Alice. 'Where shall I go? And Marianne? For he must guess how much she has to do with all this.'

'You must come to me, my dear,' said Mrs Gorman,

patting her hand. 'Geoffrey Lacey in a temper holds no fears for me. I have boxed his ears too often when he was a lad, and well he remembers it. Your mother was far too gentle with him.'

'I shall be thankful to come to you.'

'And in the meantime,' went on Mrs Gorman, 'I will write a note to Laura. Soft words butter no parsnips, and they don't hurt me to offer 'em either. I shall move in with John, and then I can keep a close eye on things. I cannot understand why Violet is so long overdue. She must have muddled up her dates, poor child—but we will not talk of that. And the house has gone to pieces! I declare the butler spends all his time over the *Morning Post* with his feet up, and the new nurserymaid dresses in white like a fine lady. Of course Violet was over young to have gotten married, but she has let things get quite out of control. John was so grateful when I offered to take some of the weight off her shoulders.'

Alice could only hope that Violet Gorman welcomed the interference as much as did her husband.

Before going to bed that night Marianne politely requested the pleasure of a few words with Laura.

'Dear Lady Lacey,' she said winningly, 'when I came to London I imagined I would be staying at this house as a guest of my cousin.'

'Do not think that you are unwelcome,' Laura replied. Since dinner she had had an unpleasant hour with her husband and felt her nerves unable to stand any more wracking that day.

'You are too kind,' Marianne told her. 'And my reception here has been everything I could wish. Nevertheless, I feel I cannot trespass on your hospitality any more.'

'Are you thinking of leaving us?' asked Laura in dismay. If Marianne—and Alice—were to depart from under her roof, not only would the house cease to be such an outstanding attraction (for the bell at the front door rang constantly and the cards on Laura's mantleshelf stood three deep), but London would say in truth that Sir Geoffrey had cast his unfortunate sister out in the world, and Laura felt that gossip was not being kind to her at present.

'Oh no. That is to say, unless you wish me to. But Lady Lacey, I must insist on taking some share of the extra expenses. Parties, horses, the use of the carriage —all this is too much for me to accept from someone who is not in fact a relation.'

'I assure you, Marianne . . .'

'I have arranged, dear Lady Lacey, that Alice's and my horses shall be sent round from Pott's livery stables, and they will also hold a carriage in readiness for us whenever we need to go out together. This will spare us from imposing too much upon you.'

'Arranged? How can you have arranged?' asked Laura, taken completely by surprise.

'Mr Percy Brown was kind enough to handle the affair for me,' Marianne told her demurely, and went on to inform the speechless Laura that she would like to contribute towards the household accounts.

Laura did not immediately reject the suggestion in the way she would have liked. Her mind was in a sad muddle over the staggering total which a cloud of bills had started to assume. She had merely indulged in a few pieces of modish furniture to replace some of Alice's old favourites and had the drawing-room done out in the latest style. A Louis XV revival had taken London by storm this year—chairs must be covered with lavish brocade, with all their woodwork carved and gilt or they were considered hopelessly behind the times; a *chaise longue* or two in matching brocade was an obvious necessity; and there was that charming bracelet that exactly matched the Lacey emeralds. Each piece in itself had been such a bargain! It should have been so easy with their new access of wealth.

106

Like her mama before her, Laura expected to remain in complete ignorance of the extent of Sir Geoffrey's income. One judged when one had overspent by the state of one's husband's wrath when he read the bills. No wrath, no overspending. And Geoffrey had been remarkably complacent at first.

But somehow she knew that the latest demands would cause him quite extravagant annoyance. Four ball dresses for herself were permissible, and the walking dress for Clara, perhaps, and the much-desired Thompson's crinolines, and the parasols, and draw-string purses, and fans, and shoes, and ribbons . . . but who could have thought that *flowers* could cost so much when you filled the house up with them regularly, or that cloth for footmen's uniforms could reach so high a sum? And this new housekeeper, who looked so much smarter than Mrs Vesey, was surely exorbitant in her demands for butcher's meat and very best butter? When Alice was mistress, did not the weekly hamper from Holt Lacey suffice?

The money coming in had more than doubled, but what flowed out went at a faster pace. And Geoffrey had always been a man of such careful habit . . .

In the end Laura found herself agreeing to a little financial arrangement with the heiress from St Kitts. It all came about so naturally. It seemed to settle itself.

'So now we are free!' Marianne told Alice. 'Let us plan the invitations for our party, Alice. Who was that very presentable young gentleman standing at the railings in the park with Captain Wargate? Is he a suitable person to be asked? Can he dance?'

'You are much more likely to find the Prime Minister coming,' replied Alice, 'if Laura can persuade him, which she will do if she can.'

'What a bore,' said Marianne St George.

CHAPTER NINE

Lady Locke conceived it to be her christian duty to guide her son in all his ways and see that he married money. Of course the young lady would be dutiful and modest, and a tolerably pretty face would be an advantage, but Lady Locke was not over-particular. Her managerial talents, suppressed for years by the domination of the late Lord Locke, had blossomed since her widowhood and enabled her to combine a strict economy with necessary social entertainment.

Her first exclamation, on hearing of the loss of Alice Lacey's expectations, had been characteristic. 'Great heavens!' cried Lady Locke in dismay. 'And I have already sent out cards for the reception!'

It was not to be a dinner party or a ball, but an elegant evening affair with music, where cake and sweet white wine were to be brought round at two hour intervals. Ladies hesitated to hold sticky cake above their best lace evening skirts, and no gentleman had ever been known to take a second glass of Lady Locke's white wine.

'There is nothing so vulgar, to my mind, as a lavish display of food and drink,' said Her Ladyship, and her son very doubtfully agreed.

Before she had thought up a credible reason for cancelling her party, Lady Locke heard that Laura Lacey wished to bring—not the original heiress—but one almost as good. She set about to find out more.

'Is she black?' the mother demanded of her son before he had time to slip off to the House of Lords, which with his clubs tended to provide the only domestic comfort available to Lord Locke.

'Is who black, Mother?'

109

'This Miss St George. The cousin of the Laceys from the Colonies?'

'Good gracious, Mother, no! Her skin is of the very whitest description.'

'And her manners? Colonial, are they, and uncouth?'

'Miss St George's behaviour is the very picture of elegance.'

'Ah— Sickly, is she? Pale and silent? All dried up with that hot sun?'

'My dear Mother, you could not be more mistaken. Miss St George is quite a beauty, and her conversation is sprightly and unforced.'

'What a pity,' said Her Ladyship candidly. 'All the men are dangling after her I suppose. She'll get her head turned and teach herself to look higher than a Colonial should. I suppose Matthew Vale is interested? They say Severn is coming down upon him hard to get himself married at last.'

'I couldn't say, Mother. I used to think he was casting eyes at Miss Alice.'

'That is all finished,' said Lady Locke immediately. 'I see Laura Lacey intends to bring Alice to my reception and I wonder that she wastes her time. However, it is none of our business. You will receive her with christian charity, Bartholomew, and leave her severely alone.'

'Yes, Mother.'

'But as to Miss St George, we must act quickly, before one of the swells cuts you out. Tell me what are the gel's special interests? I should like her to enjoy my party. And if the night is fine and you can persuade her out into the shrubbery, it would be an excellent time to pop the question.'

'I hardly know her,' said Lord Locke uncomfortably.

'Well you should!' rapped back his mother. 'With so much at stake—with all your brothers to educate and set up in the world, you should make it your business to find out what pleases a young lady like Miss St George and then do exactly what she wishes. Until you are

110

married, of course, when the positions are reversed. Is she poetical? Does she like music? Or would she appreciate an invitation to inspect the beasts in the zoological gardens?'

'The thing Miss St George really likes is dancing,' Lord Locke remembered after some wracking of his brains.

'My reception is not a ball.'

'A pity.'

'Nevertheless,' went on Her Ladyship thoughtfully, 'we could have a few strings in the corner of the large saloon. Then if the young people wished it, they could get up a few dances spontaneously.'

'They certainly would wish it, Mother.'

'Mind you don't speak of dancing beforehand, Bartholomew. It must seem to happen by accident, or people will say I ought to provide a proper band.'

'Very well, Mother.' And there the matter stayed.

'It is the greatest inconvenience,' said Marianne to Alice, 'that your sister has forbidden Mr Christopher to come to this house. There has been no word from him, has there?'

'No. But I have had no letters at all—I begin to wonder whether Laura is tampering with my mail.'

'It would be so like her. But we really must find out how Mr Christopher is progressing. These lawyers need constant harassment or they fall asleep on the job. Shall we ask Mr Christopher to meet us in the park?'

Alice smiled then laughed outright. 'Now that really would set all the tongues wagging,' she said. 'Laura would hear of it within the hour.'

'His job seems so simple,' said Marianne, who was pacing up and down the room with short, irritated steps. 'And doesn't touch the real, knotty problem at all. But what can we do? Nothing! We are only women.

111

Fit to stitch hems and play the piano. It makes me wild!'

'What do you mean by the *knotty problem*, Marianne?'

'Why, where and how your mama was wed, of course. Mr Christopher will get your fortune back—in time, of course, in man's good time—but that will not satisfy me completely—will it you, Alice?'

'No. Not at all.'

'How could it have happened? For Tante Amelie was so like you, Alice. She was the pattern of logic, and what could have been more illogical, more unreasonable, more utterly careless than to have omitted getting married when there was nothing to prevent it? I suppose Geoffrey's mother really was dead? She is not shut up secretly in a madhouse somewhere, howling at the moon?'

'Oh no. I have seen her grave in the Holt Lacey churchyard.'

'Then your parents' behaviour is a mystery and I do not like mysteries,' said Marianne. 'Where can that dressmaker have got to, Alice? It will be time for our ride soon. Listen! Let us think. At least we have the freedom to do that. Sir Walter went straight to Nevis on his first wife's death, did he not?'

'Yes.'

'And stayed only a few days, then returned direct by ship to Bristol?'

'I believe so.'

'He did not get married on the island and he was already married when the ship reached England. They must, they *must* have stopped at one of the other islands on their way—or even somewhere on the mainland like Boston.'

'Mr Christopher said they came by regular packet, and that is direct.'

'It must be checked again. If only we were men, how easy it would be! Sir Walter and your mother left Nevis

112

unmarried and reached England as man and wife. Somewhere they were wed. We only have to find *where*.'

'Marianne,' cried Alice, awestruck. 'Cannot ships' captains perform the marriage ceremony?'

'Can they?' asked Marianne, and pondered. 'Of course they can!' she cried joyfully. 'Do you not remember in the *Romance of Salerno* how George and Sylvia discovered on board ship that they are not brother and sister . . .'

' . . . and Captain Wheeler marries them to each other to stop the attentions of Count Orlandine?'

'We've got it!' shouted Marianne, flinging herself upon Alice. 'That's it! Your parents were married on the ship coming to England. Hurray!' And the two girls spun round the room to the great alarm of Phoebe, who brought a message to say that the dressmaker was indisposed and could not be with them that day.

'Well now we simply must see Mr Christopher again,' said Marianne. 'And soon. Let us ask Mr Vale to arrange a meeting.'

'No.'

'Then what do you suggest? Upon my honour, Alice, one of my greatest wishes in coming to London was to get away from the restraints that bind a young lady in Basseterre. Even for a short while, I thought, it would be delightful to be free. But we are hedged about here —in spite of a huge society—far worse than I was at home. I could at least consult an attorney at Beauregarde without anyone raising a finger of shame.'

'We could ask him to call at some house where we visit,' Alice said thoughtfully. 'I think my godmother would let him come when we were there ourselves.'

'Yes, and frighten young Mrs Gorman into such a fit that she produced a monster!' cried Marianne. 'Would not your friend Lady Arthur give us cover?'

'I doubt it. It would embarrass me to ask such a thing.'

'Then we shall not ask!' cried Marianne, flinging

113

wide her hands. 'Phooo! How these restrictions erk me! We will tell Mr Christopher to come to some house— any house—where we are engaged to be, and it will be easy to have a few words with him.'

'What hostess who we know would invite him into her house for a party?'

'Then *outside* the house! Oh, how I hate all these contradictions! If you get back your fortune, Alice, you won't have deserved it one little bit! Why don't you help, instead of putting up all these objections?'

'I'm sorry, Marianne, it just does not seem poss- ible ...'

'Then we will *make* it possible. Where are we invited next, Alice? Lord Locke's, is it not? What a dreary prospect! If he asks me to waltz I shall pretend that I have ricked my ankle—no, that would not do, for then I could not dance with anybody else.'

'There will be no dancing, Marianne. We shall be offered improving conversation and precious little else, if I know Lady Locke.'

'All the more reason for enlivening the affair, then. We will write to Mr Christopher—Phoebe can take the letter—and request him to meet us there. Is there some deserted library or office we could use? You know the house, do you not, Alice? And please take that prunes- and-prisms look off your face or I shall lose all interest in your affairs, I swear it.'

Alice laughed. 'Oh, how I would love to see Lady Locke's face if she knew you were making assignations under her roof,' she cried. 'She is a perfect old dragon and had fixed on me to be an obedient daughter-in-law when I was rich. How she persuaded herself that I was the sort of person she admired, when common sense must show her we would be like Kilkenny cats after a week of living together, I cannot think.'

'I like hopeful mamas as a rule,' said Marianne. 'They are all so anxious to be pleased. Now where shall we tell Mr Christopher to meet us? You don't know a back way, do you Alice, by which he could enter? Is there a straggle of stables where we could be unseen?'

'No. It is a remarkably square and matter-of-fact place set against Regent's Park,' Alice said, knitting her brows. 'It has no outbuildings that I can remember. Indeed it is entirely surrounded by its own garden and the shrubberies are famous. People often wander in from the park to enjoy them.'

'Shrubberies!' cried Marianne. 'The very thing! I will tell Mr Christopher that we will meet him in the shrubberies behind Locke Place. And then he can pretend—if we are discovered—that he is just a passer-by.'

Alice did not try to thwart her. She guessed that Matthew Vale would pull them out of a scrape if Marianne's impetuosity landed them in one. She knew he would be present at the reception, because he had already told her so.

Matthew Vale was deeply troubled. The son of an invalid, his mother had died whilst he was still young, and he had been brought up very much under the influence of the Duke of Severn. Till now he had found the duke's comfortable way of life—entirely indifferent to the Mrs Grundies of this world and spent much abroad—quite to his own tastes, though these were not naturally so extravagant as those of his august relative. He did not want to end his days, however, in a lonely glitter like the duke's last years, where smiles from pretty faces depended upon regular gifts of jewelled trinkets, and he had been prepared for some time to oblige His Grace by marrying and setting up a family. He would like to have boys of his own whom he could raise with more love and attention than had ever fallen his own way, and was prepared to offer for any lady of sufficient beauty and adequate breeding. A fortune would be welcome, as it would make him more independent of the duke, but it was not essential, and for several years,

115

when his parliamentary duties brought him to town, Matthew Vale had attended the Social Season with a heart quite ready to be captured by any young lady with the wit to set about it properly.

If only the young ladies had not been so abominably obliging!

Each girl, it seemed to him, each female shoot that sprung from English county stock, was trained from birth by her mama to be a—a—a—smothering mass of pink-flowered bindweed.

Surely, to love, to honour and to obey was enough, without making a fetish out of it?

The poets were very much to blame. Matthew did not read poetry himself, but he had a feeling that girls nowadays lingered far too long on stanzas about devotion and immolation and noble sacrifices and pesky moated granges. That fellow Tennyson—dammit, you could not enter a drawing-room without finding a young lady poring over his works. And what was the result? Each longed to be a clinging vine, a loving, tender, all-embracing plant forever putting out soft tendrils with one iron intent; to clasp, to cling, to entwine, to adore and to penetrate every fibre of a husband's being.

He doubted, quite candidly, whether he had the stamina to bear it. No sooner would he direct his gaze at some personable young woman, than she would lean softly towards him, as if her whole future longed to hang itself upon his strength. Sometimes the ballrooms of London seemed to Matthew Vale to be fields of sweet-pea seedlings waiting for sturdy sticks to climb up, and when this picture overcame him, he would retire to Severn Abbey with a few cronies and behave perhaps more wildly than his nature inclined him to. The duke had no objection, and it broke that unpleasant sensation of green tendrils that Matthew could not bear.

This season, however, had presented something quite new in Mr Vale's experience. The name of Alice Lacey meant little to him except as the daughter of a neigh-

116

bour at Severn Abbey—a muddy, frightened, schoolgirl whom he had once pulled out of a brook. He had cast one of his usual sardonic glances her way when she was launched into society. And then he had looked again. And again. He had liked what he saw. He had been amused by the calm, unruffled way she disposed of suitors who did not appeal to her, and had admired her very capable handling of her own large affairs. He had talked to her, and found her ready to be interested. When she lifted her eyes to his face, he had met a frank, steady gaze entirely different from those soulful looks that sent him half across a room. Here was one, he felt, who could be trusted to look after the female side of a man's estate—even a dukedom—without demanding to be told her husband was enjoying every mouthful of his dinner, and to arrange her life pleasantly so that it was not blighted for ever if the man of the house was called upon to pass a late night in the House or spend his November days in the hunting field.

So Matthew's conscious mind had informed him. Unconsciously, he found himself attending social functions much more often than he used to, staying longer, dancing more and gravitating without fail to the corner of the room where the female Laceys were established. He became truly offended when Alice could only spare one waltz for him, furious with fellows who hung over her immoderately, and aggrieved if he attended a function where she was not also present. These feelings had grown upon him before he was aware of them, and left his critical judgment far behind.

However, when Alice ceased to be an eligible *parti*, Mr Vale's one thought should have been profound relief that he had kept his growing intentions to himself. He was entirely dependent on his uncle's favour for the very clothes that he stood up in, and he knew very well the high opinion which the duke had of good blood. Were he to offer the old man a niece born out of wedlock, His Grace would instantly cast him off, and he had

117

no means of subsistence beyond his allowance. For the first time in his life Matthew cursed the careless way in which he had accepted the pleasant mode of life that had been pressed upon him. If only he had chosen to go into the law or the army—or even the church. But at that thought he grinned. He did not feel he was at all suited to the church.

Yet imagine, if he was the incumbent of a comfortable living, with a curate to do all the work and a fine disdain for those who disapproved of hunting parsons, at least he would have had a home to offer a wife. His uncle would have been surprised, but a well-paid benefice would have fallen into his lap as easily as had the parliamentary seat for Six Mile Severn, and for a moment Matthew indulged in the blissful picture of a cosy rural rectory, himself coming in from the stables, and Alice bending over her work near the fire in all the trappings of simple domestic comfort so lovingly described by Mr Dickens.

Then he pulled himself together. This would not do. He must be practical, and Matthew prided himself on being a practical man. He was willing—anxious—to help Alice as far as friendship required. He would further her interests with this law suit—but the result of that would be a compromise, he suspected, which would give her a small independence if things went well. Nothing could make her birth acceptable to the duke, even if she were to get her old fortune back again *in toto*. He would help her, just that, and then withdraw from the acquaintance and revert to his old, enjoyable ways again, and some time—in the near future, for the duke was becoming quite pressing—he would submit to those soft green tentacles which seemed so much like steel bands.

Then a breeze of madness swept over him. Why did he not go to Alice now, and offer his heart, even if it meant losing everything? A heart is all very well, but they could not live on it. When other men made dis-

118

astrous marriages, they set up house cheaply on the continent in places like Boulogne, but Matthew could not even do that. He would have to go and skin sheep in Australia or pack preserved meat on the plains of Paraguay, and how could that possibly benefit Alice?

'I don't know what's gotten into Mr Vale tonight,' said the Severn butler to the housekeeper that evening. 'Bit my head off when I asked him if he wanted a hot supper, and slammed right out into the night.'

'E'll 'ave gone to Kate 'Amilton's pleasure 'ouse in Panton Street,' suggested the pantry boy with a knowing leer. 'All the nobs goes there.'

'Now don't you go saying things about your betters as ain't true,' snapped an upper footman loftily, and the whole female part of the establishment—cook, parlour-maids, housemaids, chambermaids and kitchen maids—united to put the pantry boy in his place. For Mr Vale was well-liked and respected below stairs, unlike the Duke of Severn, who would sack a woman of fourteen years service if his linen was not ironed to his satisfaction.

'I don't know why Mr Vale has to go outside the 'ouse to seek his pleasures, that I don't,' sighed a dreamy-eyed kitchen tweeny, and was promptly sat upon by the entire staff.

CHAPTER TEN

That most prudent of mamas, Lady Locke, had had no idea of the effect of an impromptu dance upon a large set of people who had come prepared for music and conversation. In London at the height of the Season, on the first really warm night of the year, it opened up possibilities that she had not foreseen. Ballroom behaviour was strictly understood. Young ladies knew where they should be at each part of the evening, and at what points they were expected to be found at their mothers' sides.

With dancing in the large saloon, however, and conversation in the drawing-rooms, Madame Patti carolling away in the long gallery for the musically-minded and a delicious sunset gilding the gardens, mamas found their daughters disappearing in one direction or another for perfectly satisfactory reasons, but without much chance of being found.

Alice was almost immediately separated from Marianne's side and, after some dancing, she was trapped in a corner by Mr Bunne. As far as she knew, her cousin had been borne off to see Lord Locke's collection of minerals.

'I have been most anxious to see you again,' Mr Bunne cried, 'and to tell you that I have been approached by a most worthy society to act as its secretary and deal with the large correspondence. It has made me so happy and I was sure, Miss Alice, that you would join in my pleasure.'

'Indeed yes, Mr Bunne,' she replied politely. 'This is some society for work in the mission field, I take it?'

'No, it is much nearer home. In the very heart of our city,' Mr Bunne told her with great enthusiasm, 'and its purpose is the reclamation of the souls of fallen women and their restoration to some work suitable to their degree.'

'How interesting,' said Alice, her eyes searching the room for Marianne. Their appointment in the shrubbery was at an early hour, and she did not want to leave the house alone.

'It is indeed one of the greatest calls that has ever been made upon me,' said Mr Bunne, much gratified. 'And I knew you would feel exactly the same about it as I do, dear Miss Alice. I cannot, of course, ask for your active help on this subject, as some of the details,' he peered into her face with his innocent eyes quite goggling behind their spectacles, 'are quite unfit for female ears. But the thought of your approval will be a strong encouragement to me to continue with the work.'

It had begun to dawn upon Alice that Mr Bunne only needed the very slightest encouragement to be brought to look upon her as a cause which he could worthily take up. Indeed, he was more than halfway there himself. It would give him profound pleasure, Alice guessed, to feel that in proposing marriage he was performing an act of disinterested charity, and one part of Alice's nature felt a surge of gratitude, whilst the rest shrank in amused distaste. She far preferred the frank, monetary assessment of a Lady Locke to the philanthropic ardour which would turn her into the means of spiritual improvement to some man of more idealism than sense.

'I wish you every success in your endeavours,' Alice assured him with a certain chill in her voice and a straightening of the shoulder and tightening of her mouth which she hoped Mr Bunne would find thoroughly repulsive. Unfortunately he took it for disapproval of the subject which he had had the temerity to raise.

'My dear Miss Alice!' he cried apologetically. 'Forgive me if—dear, dear—I should have thought . . .'

But Matthew Vale was passing and bowed to Alice,

giving her the opportunity of escaping from her corner and asking anxiously, 'Have you seen Miss St George?'

'Half an hour ago, dancing with young Hawke,' Mr Vale replied.

'I will go and find her,' Alice said.

'She's not there now. A giggle of schoolgirls is performing the schottische, and I am sure Miss St George is not among them. Do you need her so badly?'

'We were to have met Mr Christopher,' Alice replied.

'*Here?*' Matthew looked really surprised.

'In the shrubbery,' Alice explained absentmindedly, as her eyes continued their search for her cousin.

'How very original!' exclaimed Mr Vale.

Alice's eyes stopped their search and went quickly up to his face. 'Whatever made me tell you?' she asked herself crossly. 'I can assure you I do not *wish* to behave myself in such an unseemly way, Mr Vale.'

'I can believe you,' he said. 'The plan has every mark of Miss St George about it. But will I not do as an escort?' She looked at him doubtfully.

'I do not wish you to get involved,' she said.

He did not wish it either, but how was he to resist a chance of driving away that small, worried furrow from between such expressive eyes?

'I will at least go with you into the garden,' he said. 'We may find Miss St George waiting for you there.'

The still evening air and the slanting rays of a pretty sunset had drawn many people out from the wide French windows on to the terrace, from where a step took them on to dry lawns and three steps into the cover of laurel and lantana bushes. Mamas would think one was dancing, after all, or listening to the strains of an Italian song. The terrace showed no sign of Marianne, however, and Alice paused, completely at a loss what to do next. 'I do not wish to keep you from dancing, Mr Vale,' she said.

'Believe me,' he replied sincerely, 'I would rather be with you.' And then wished he had not spoken. Mr Vale had quite a stock of soft nothings to whisper in ladies' ears at appropriate times. It was a change to find himself biting back words he really wanted to speak.

They both turned back towards the house. Their arms touched and then hastily drew back. He frowned, Alice blushed. They traversed the length of the house at a decorous distance from each other and entered the conservatory in the manner of very distant friends.

As they walked down its length under Lady Locke's choicest palms and potted plants, there was a slight scuffle at the far end, a small shriek and the handsome form of Captain Wargate sprang back from behind a fine specimen of *dieffenbachia picta*.

'Great heavens!' cried Matthew Vale. 'Is anything amiss, Wargate?' For the captain's face was flushed.

'Did you kill it?' enquired Marianne's voice, slightly higher pitched than usual. 'Oh is that you, Alice? I was looking for you, but you would not have arrived in time to save me from a dreadful fate. Fortunately Captain Wargate was able to do so.'

'Dreadful fate?' asked Alice.

'Yes. A tropical spider,' Marianne told her, standing on tiptoes and peering all round the huge hem of her dress with every sign of alarm. 'You did kill it, did you not Captain Wargate? It fell on my shoulder as I was passing these horrible plants. A huge, hairy green thing —perhaps a green widow. Is there such an insect as a green widow in England? Is its bite fatal? I was quite helpless. No doubt you heard me scream.'

There was no reason why a green spider on the shoulder should crush the rose on one's bosom, but Alice felt no call to comment on this when they left the flustered Captain Wargate and the amused Matthew Vale and stepped out on to the gravel path which swept up the side of Locke Place and disappeared into the shrubbery.

'I do hope that Mr Christopher will not have got tired of waiting,' Alice said. 'We are half an hour after the

124

time you mentioned, Marianne.' They plunged in among the bushes and lost sight of the house.

'The park lies at the far end,' said Alice, and they tried to find their way through a veritable maze. 'Oh! Did you see that?' she whispered in dismay.

'It was only young Mrs Larraby-Turnbull. What splendid whiskers her husband has.'

'That was not Mr Larraby-Turnbull, Marianne.'

The heiress giggled. 'What a delightful place this is,' she said, as they passed from path to glade and on to secluded arbour, and then paused beside a chaste white marble nymph to look round in approval. Four paths disappeared in four different directions, and each curved quickly out of sight. 'Who would have thought Lord Locke would cherish such an enchanting shrubbery? I would have expected him to cut it down.'

'Please speak quietly, Marianne,' whispered Alice. 'We cannot tell if we are overheard.' A sudden turn of the path brought before her a hasty glimpse of a young lady who should have been beside her mama.

'Miss St George!' came a ghostly voice unseen, almost as if it had caught her words. 'Is that you? Are you not in danger of catching cold in the open so late in the evening?'

'Percy Brown,' mouthed Alice in horror, and she and Marianne darted another way. By the greatest good luck, Marianne saw the form of Mr Christopher at the bottom of a path where only a thin fringe of bushes separated the garden from the park.

'There he is!' she cried.

'I did not think you had seen me!' was the pleased reply, and Percy Brown appeared from a side path. 'You are very sharp-eyed, Miss St George!'

'Am I?' she asked, momentarily non-plussed.

'Very. I have been following you since you entered this place in case I could be of service in leading you back to the house again. Shall I do so? Lady Lacey will be worried if she looks for you on the dance floor and cannot find you.'

'What I really need, Mr Brown, is my shawl,' said Marianne confidingly. 'Would you be so *very* kind as to bring it for me? I feel I must have a little fresh air, but it is rather shady in this nice peaceful place. Would you get it, Mr Brown? It is with Phoebe, my maid, you know. She was sitting in the cloakroom when last I saw her.'

'I will be as quick as I can!' cried Percy and ran off to execute his lady's commission.

'Oh Mr Christopher!' Alice ran down the path towards him. 'We have thought of an answer to the whole question. It explains everything.'

'We think,' said Marianne, 'that Sir Walter and Lady Lacey would have been married by the ship's captain on their voyage to England.'

'Does that not seem very likely to you?' demanded Alice. 'It would account for all the things which have been difficult to understand.'

'Alice, is that you?' came a voice to the right of them. 'Have you seen Clara?'

'*Laura!*' hissed Marianne, and pushed Mr Christopher into the welcoming arms of a golden laurel just as Lady Lacey came into view.

'I cannot understand it,' she complained. 'She was dancing with Mr Hawke and then I saw her with a crowd of young people ...'

'Let me go with you to find her,' suggested Marianne, seizing Laura's wrist with one hand and pushing Alice so firmly back against the golden laurel with the other that her crinoline billowed forward.

'Thank you,' said Laura, gratified.

'Are you there, my love?'

The form of Sir Geoffrey now appeared from the park side looking angry and heated. 'I cannot think where the tiresome child has gone,' he declared.

'You stay here with Alice, while we go and look for

her,' said Laura. 'Oh, I am sorry, Mr Vale. I did not see that you were there.'

'Is anything the matter?' Matthew asked as Marianne and Laura hurried away.

'Evening, Vale. What do you think of our chances with the Church Bill?' Sir Geoffrey asked, easing his collar.

'It might go to a second reading,' said Matthew Vale, deliberately turning so that Geoffrey had to face him. 'But if it does, they will cut it about so much in committee that we shall not recognize it. What do you think yourself?' He had caught the desperate appeal in Alice's eyes and had not missed the sudden jerk of two golden laurel twigs. The face that he offered to Sir Geoffrey was perfectly sober, but his shoulders twitched under their well-cut coat.

'I think we should have left it till the next session,' Sir Geoffrey said, 'and trusted that all the opposition would die down.'

'Miss Alice! I have been looking for you everywhere,' came a fresh voice, and Mr Bunne trotted into the little circular area where they were standing at the junction of several paths. He was even hotter than Sir Geoffrey, and pulled out a handkerchief to mop his brow as he pressed forward with single-minded intent. 'Excuse me, Vale. Miss Alice, did I offend you? I should have thought before I spoke. I have been dismayed . . .' and he scrubbed his damp forehead with the handkerchief.

'There was nothing to cause the smallest offence, Mr Bunne,' said Alice, not stepping forward to greet him. Mr Christopher was ominously quiet behind her. She hoped he had not impaled himself upon a branch.

'The subject matter is a trifle delicate,' went on Mr Bunne, 'but the task is a noble one. Come, Miss Alice, let me conduct you to the house and explain how we are planning to bring these unfortunate females back into a life of respectability.'

'Now where is Miss St George?' demanded Percy, who had come back with Marianne's shawl.

'She is with Laura,' said Alice, trying to catch Matthew's eye. If only he could somehow relieve her of Mr Bunne.

Matthew did not fail. 'They went towards the house,' he said. 'We shall find them on the terrace. You had better hurry, Brown, or the lady might catch cold. Lacey, will you lead the way? Bunne, perhaps you will go before me.'

The strength of his personality was such that all three gentlemen had turned away and gone into a narrow path, and Alice had stepped forward thankfully when Laura arrived by a different route dragging an unwilling Clara behind her. 'Is that you, Geoffrey?' demanded his wife. 'Could you please have the carriage called. I have had quite enough of this evening.'

'I don't want to go home yet,' said Clara Brown in the manner of a spoilt child.

'Stop pulling at my arm!' her sister told her. 'You had no business to be talking with Mr Hawke alone.'

'We were all right until you and Marianne came up,' said Clara crossly.

'Where *is* Miss St George?' asked Percy Brown, trying to peer over Mr Vale's tall shoulder and not succeeding.

A tiny scream came from the all-concealing shrubs quite close at hand.

Alice took a startled step forward. Percy Brown cried, 'I am coming!' in a very dramatic way, and Mr Bunne turned puzzled spectacles in every direction.

'Geoffrey!' cried Laura in tones of horror. 'There is a man lurking in the bushes.'

'Nonsense, my dear. You are imagining things.'

'It's not nonsense,' said Laura, 'and I think I am going to faint.'

'Come out, sir, and make yourself known!' cried the valiant Mr Bunne.

'Let us take the ladies to the house for safety,' said

128

Matthew Vale. 'Lady Lacey, your arm. Miss Brown, Miss Alice, come.'

'Oh there you are Alice, I have been searching and searching to find this place again,' cried Marianne, fluttering up and taking in the situation at a glance, 'And I am quite worn out . . . my constitution . . . Sir Geoffrey, can you give me support? Lady Lacey do you have your salts with you? Clara can you lend me a fan?'

Enough agitation was caused to enable Mr Christopher to slide away towards the park, but unfortunately, in leaving he brushed past Mr Percy Brown who was hurrying their way.

'Who was that?' demanded Percy suspiciously.

'Oh! Have you got my shawl, Mr Brown? How very kind! Please let me have it. Oh! I do not know when I have been so fatigued,' gasped Marianne.

'I'm sure I've seen that fellow's face before,' said Sir Geoffrey.

'Come, Miss St George, I will help you to the house,' said Matthew, taking her arm firmly and leading her away. Geoffrey took Clara's arm and followed straight behind.

'I know who it was—it was the attorney who visited us in Portman Square!' said Lady Lacey in bewilderment rather than anger. Then, see Mr Bunne about to offer himself as an escort for Alice, she took his arm and propelled him towards the terrace.

Percy Brown turned on Alice. 'You *arranged* to meet him here!' he accused her.

Profoundly thankful that Marianne had written the note, Alice permitted herself a denial.

'Then Miss St George did,' he surmised darkly. 'It can come to no good, Miss Alice.'

Alice turned and started to follow the others.

'And if I get my hands on that young Hawke, it shall go hard with him,' muttered Percy as he walked behind.

CHAPTER ELEVEN

'Marianne,' said Alice, when the two girls were sitting dressed for a party and waiting for Laura and Clara to be ready, 'may I ask you a question?'

'But of course.'

'A very—er—personal question?'

'Well yes, Alice. Please go on. I do not have to answer, after all.'

'Then tell me . . . why do you scream?'

'I do not understand you,' said the heiress blankly.

'I cannot understand *you*. It seems to me,' Alice explained awkwardly, 'that either the—er—attentions of a gentleman are unwelcome, in which case one states so quite plainly, or else they are received with pleasure. And in that case, naturally one indicates that he must speak to one's papa. What I cannot comprehend is why you scream as though a—an approach is distasteful, yet seem to do nothing to prevent it happening again.'

Marianne, who was perched on the bed, fell over on her face in a cloud of giggles and flounces. 'Dear Alice,' she proclaimed, 'you are always so utterly logical.'

'But is not what I say true?' asked Alice, hurt.

'Well, yes—and no. That is, you are talking about life as people say it is, but not as things actually are.'

'Now I have no idea what you mean.'

Marianne giggled again.

'I could understand your being shocked, or frightened or unhappy or surprised—indeed under some circumstances I realize one would be overwhelmingly content,' said poor Alice. 'But,' she pulled herself out of an incipient daydream, 'I cannot understand a *scream*.'

Marianne gave a deep sigh and turned her mind to the matter. 'It is something to do with Great-Aunt Euphemie,' she said at last.

131

'I beg your pardon?' This was the last thing Alice had expected.

'Well you see,' said Marianne thoughtfully, 'when a gentleman starts showing by his behaviour that he is not entirely indifferent—that he is *attracted* would perhaps be a better word . . .'

'Then he is expected to think well about his intentions and if his state of life and inclinations lead him to the idea of marriage . . .'

'No, no. There you go again Alice. So logical, as I said before. I am talking about something that can arise without any thought of marriage at all.'

Alice turned round in her chair to stare. 'I hope I do not understand you correctly,' she said.

'No. We will not pursue the subject, for I fear you might start lecturing me. But about the scream, Alice, I can only say—when all my senses are just about to reach the peak of gratification, suddenly the face of Great-Aunt Euphemie comes between me and the gentleman concerned, and at the very moment when he—er—leans over me, I am smitten with a great gust of horror. So I scream.'

'Great heavens!' cried Alice. 'What a dreadful thing.'

'Well yes, in a way. Except that it makes it more enjoyable. And of course the gentlemen take it for modesty and become very much confused.'

'I think,' said Alice cautiously, 'that I should prefer my pleasure unalloyed.'

'Ah, yes, but there you see Alice, you are so logical, as we agreed before.' They looked at each other, laughed, and Alice thought it was time to change the subject.

'I would not have you think me inquisitive,' she said, 'but sometimes one is forced to think of the future, and it is impossible to tell from your behaviour, dearest Marianne, whether you are planning to marry and settle in England or to return unmarried to the West Indies. Do you know yourself?'

132

The heiress put the tip of her index finger to her mouth and nibbled it delicately.

'I am sorry. I had no right to ask,' said Alice, contrite.

'It is rather difficult . . .' began Marianne, when Alice signalled her to stop.

'Nobody shall force your confidence, and least of all myself, when you have been such a good friend to me,' she said. 'Only, if you do happen to return to St Kitts, it was in my mind to ask you whether I might perhaps go with you. Now that Frenchman's Point is actually mine—thanks to your generosity—I should very much like to inspect it and see if I can perhaps live there and make it prosper.'

'Dearest Alice!' cried Marianne immediately. 'Of course you can always command a home with me! And do not think of hiding yourself away on Nevis. The plantation is quite incapable of improvement. It is bounded on three sides by the sea and has never re-covered from the hurricane of '46. Even if the soil were as fertile as St Kitts, which it is not, Frenchman's Point does not have the acreage to support its own factory, and no plantation can ever profit beyond a certain limit when it depends upon the neighbours for its existence. You shall go to Beauregarde whenever I do myself and, though the society at Basseterre is limited, we should find enough to keep ourselves amused. Only—I should like to remain in England some time longer. It is my last chance, you see.'

Alice went over to Marianne and kissed her. 'I shall not plant myself upon you in St Kitts or England if I can help it,' she promised, 'but it is kind of you to ask me and gives me a great deal of comfort. For it would be impossible for me to stay with Geoffrey and Laura after you go, and there is no alternative, it seems, be-tween that and my godmother's house in the country . . .'

'. . . or marriage to Mr Bunne and the Philanthropic Society!' suggested Marianne impertinently.

'I shall marry Mr Bunne, my dear Marianne, on the day that you marry Mr Percy Brown.'

'Alas, that will never be. Mr Brown has found me out. He thinks I am a contriving minx with no sense of proper behaviour.'

'Fiddlesticks! He thinks the sun shines out of your eyes.'

'No longer. Ah me! He caught me on my way up-stairs from lunch today, and how he had changed!'

'Did he speak to you?'

'Speak to me? He read me the riot act. He said I was shaming my sex and sullying my name and disgracing the very spirit of maidenhood.'

'Heavens and earth! For what reason?'

'For arranging a clandestine meeting with a low attorney.'

Alice's cheeks glowed angrily. 'You should have boxed his ears,' she said.

'I was tempted,' Marianne admitted, 'but it is useful for the moment to have him as a friend. I wept.'

'You *what*?'

'I melted. I said I was so, so sorry. I told him how difficult it was for young ladies to do anything at all in this wicked world without a strong arm to protect them. I told him I was driven to do bad things because I was quite alone. It was so sad I nearly made him weep. I said that I hated any form of business because it made my poor head ache.'

'Marianne!'

'Perhaps I overdid it a little. He looked quite stunned.'

'As well he might.'

Alice was wearing one of her prettiest dresses that evening. It was of sprigged muslin with five deep flounces, and though muslin was not worn any longer in the daytime, it had never lost its hold on evening wear. In default of a brooch, she had pinned real roses to her bodice and was conscious of looking well. The

134

possibility of a shipboard marriage between her parents had raised a glow of hope that she could not quite suppress and it was inevitable that she should look happy.

When they returned from the party, it was to find an upset in the house. Sir Geoffrey had not gone with them, for the House had sat till eleven o'clock and then he had returned home via his club. He had then found a tall black figure standing in the hall surrounded by a milling mass of household staff. An old man with a frizzled mop of white hair, wrapped up to his ears in an ancient greatcoat and a quantity of shawls, stood dumb and bewildered, not understanding the questions that were being fired at him from all sides.

'What is this?' asked Geoffrey crossly. The once well-run household, he was unable to ignore, was disintegrating under Laura's management, and he was coming to realize that though Alice's servants might have lacked the hard glitter of high fashion, they thoroughly knew the business of supplying steady comfort to their employers.

'What is it?' repeated Sir Geoffrey testily. There did not seem anybody capable of giving him a sensible answer.

'Oh Sir!' cried one of the new footmen who had only started work that week, 'he called me *master*, fancy that!'

'The poor benighted heathen!' exclaimed the new housekeeper.

'It's the only word he knows, it seems,' said the parlourmaid. 'He called Mr Jenkins *master* too.'

'They shouldn't have sent him such a long way on his own. 'Tes cruel, with him so old and all,' added cook, who looked as though she had been roused from her bed.

'Hold him up, John, do, he's fair amazed with all the lights,' commanded the head housemaid of the footman, as the newcomer seemed about to droop.

'What in heaven's name is going on?' demanded Sir Geoffrey Lacey.

'You stand back, Sarah, and let the master see,' commanded the butler, and a small space was cleared whereby Sir Geoffrey was able to study the tall thin figure of an old man with a wrinkled black face and a sweet, troubled expression.

'Master?' he said hopefully, hearing Sir Geoffrey's commanding voice.

'What the deuce?' wondered the baronet.

He came off a ship, they told him. A young sailor had brought him from the docks and dumped him, almost without explanation, in the house. He was consigned to Miss Alice from the West Indies. No—it was to Miss St George that he had been sent. Just look at his bundle, Sir Geoffrey, it was all wet from the sea. He had a paper —the butler had seen it—but he wouldn't say a word. Couldn't speak, most like, except one of them heathen languages. Did Master feel it was safe to let an outlandish creature like that into a christian British home? The very youngest kitchenmaid started to whimper.

'Silence!' thundered Sir Geoffrey. He dismissed the maids to their rooms and demanded to see the 'paper' which the old man had brought with him. It was coaxed from the inside pocket of an outdated, flowered-silk waistcoat. Sir Geoffrey took it, smoothed out the wrinkles, and with difficulty read, 'Joseph Lestrange, consigned to Miss St George at the house of Miss Lacey in Portman Square, London, England.'

'So you *are* meant to come here,' Sir Geoffrey said, staring at the old man. 'I thought at first it was all a mistake.'

'What are we to do with him till Miss comes home?' asked the butler.

'Oh take him away, give him food, put him by the kitchen fire—he looks half-starved,' said Sir Geoffrey indifferently. 'And bring me some cold meat and wine to my study immediately. I haven't dined tonight.'

136

'Would you like some hot soup, sir?'

'Never mind. The meat will do with bread.'

'Very good, sir. John, pick up his bundle and take it downstairs. He'll follow you fast enough when he sees that go.'

It was one o'clock before the ladies of the family returned home, and the unfortunate John had been detailed to wait up and open the door for them.

Phoebe had accompanied her mistress, who always had to have her maid at hand in case a flounce was trodden on or a curl became unpinned, and Laura's maid came sleepily upstairs from where she had been dozing in the housekeeper's room.

'There now, you forgot to bring the heathen,' John rebuked the maid.

'What heathen?' asked Alice automatically.

'John, your necktie is disgracefully loose,' said Laura instantly, jealous of her position as mistress of the house.

'An old black man, Miss, come from foreign parts,' John told Alice. 'Sent to Miss St George like a parcel, and no more to get out of him than if he was a parcel.'

'Now who can that be?' wondered Marianne. 'It is far too soon for a message to come from Great-Aunt Euphemie—she will barely have received my letters herself. Perhaps a friend in Basseterre has sent some commission . . .' and Phoebe was ordered below stairs to bring the old man up.

A tremendous cackle of greetings and cries and laughter rose from the kitchen quarters, and when Phoebe returned to the hall, she was accompanied by a grinning, happy Josephus very different from the frightened man who had confronted Sir Geoffrey earlier.

'What for you go wear the old master's coat?' Phoebe was asking him. 'You go set up for gentleman now, Josephus?' and she cackled like a hen.

'Ah, Mistress!' he cried, rushing up to Marianne, bowing low and seizing her hand.

'What for you come this place so far away, Josephus?'

137

demanded Marianne rapidly. 'How come you go for ship one person so old then? And Mistress Euphemie? She go for sick?' They chattered together in a form of English that was unintelligible to their listeners. Laura and Clara, who were tired already, listened for a few minutes and then excused themselves. 'No doubt we can hear your news in the morning, Marianne,' Laura said. 'But would it not have been simpler for your aunt to have sent a letter?'

However Great-Aunt Euphemie had sent letters. As soon as Laura and Clara had disappeared upstairs with the maid, old Josephus opened his coat and from a large interior pocket produced a roll of papers carefully stitched into a cotton bag.

'Oh dear,' said Marianne, receiving it with a grimace. 'Nine parts of this will be a sermon.'

'Could it not be about my mother?' asked Alice wistfully.

'Not by any means,' Marianne said. 'The letters which I wrote my aunt will hardly have reached St Kitts. We cannot expect an answer for four weeks or more.'

'Then let us go to bed, for I am exhausted,' said Alice.

'Yes, we will. I shall read these in the morning. Phoebe make you sleep for my room tonight and give Josephus your bed. And do not bring me tea until ten o'clock tomorrow. Come on, Alice.'

CHAPTER TWELVE

When Alice joined Marianne, as had become their custom, for breakfast in her room and to chat about the previous night's party, she found her cousin wearing a very becoming cap and opening a small three-cornered note.

'He will meet us in the park,' said Marianne with satisfaction.

'Good morning, Phoebe,' said Alice. 'How is Josephus this morning? And who will meet us in the park, Marianne?'

'He still for sleeping, Mistress. He very sick for stomach from that ship.'

'Good. Sleep is the surest remedy. Marianne, the last thing I want to do is carp, but you know very well that nothing will destroy a reputation faster than accepting assignation notes from a gentleman.'

'Well, I take that most unkindly,' said Marianne, 'when it is all about your business. And how you can face kidneys in the morning is beyond me altogether. Take them away, Phoebe, and bring me a boiled egg. I would give ten years of my life for a long, cool slice of paw-paw.'

'I see you haven't opened Aunt Euphemie's letters yet,' said Alice, nodding to the cotton-covered roll. The stitches had been half cut and then left abandoned.

'No. I know precisely what she will say,' Marianne said, 'and I shall find it exceedingly tedious. Rather like you,' she added pointedly, 'and your incessant care for my reputation.'

'I am sorry,' said Alice. 'Heaven forbid that I should become like Great-Aunt Euphemie! Tell me whom we are meeting in the park, Marianne. Is it Mr Christopher?'

'No,' said Marianne. 'I could not hope to escape notice this time with Percy Brown behaving like a dragon. I had to use a responsible go-between.'

'And who did you choose?' asked Alice, smiling.

'Mr Matthew Vale,' replied Marianne blandly.

Phoebe's entrance with the egg allowed Alice to step backwards and the slight movement masked a sudden stab of dismay. Was Marianne using Alice's problems to capture Mr Vale's interest for herself? Was it not Marianne's arm, not Alice's, that he had taken in the maze behind Locke Place?

She tried to quell such a disloyal suspicion. But why should it even be disloyal? Marianne was genuinely helping Alice. This need not run counter to a personal desire to be a wealthy duchess. Alice moved to the window and peered into the square, unseeing. There was a sort of horrible suitability about the match, she realized. Old Severn would welcome it, for the St Georges went back to the highest old French nobility, and Marianne's wealth would ensure a comfortable life for the couple until the duke was called to the family vault.

Alice gave herself a little shake. How could she harbour these ungrateful thoughts about Marianne—the only person in the world who was giving her the staunch, partisan help she needed? She looked back at the bed. Marianne was curled like a kitten over her teacup, and a French novel had replaced the little note. Her mouth smiled, the little lace petals on the edge of her cap quivered, and it all presented a delightfully child-like scene.

But Marianne had greater hidden strength as Alice well knew and unorthodox means of getting her own way. And her ambitions were quite unknown to Alice. Why should she not wish to settle in England as the future Duchess of Severn? Nothing could be more natural.

'You are not eating, Alice. You must keep your strength up, you know,' Marianne said, glancing up,

140

and Alice came over to the bedside table. Dear, kind Marianne, always so considerate! What a pity it was impossible to see the plans going on inside that exquisite little head!

'Shall I open the sermons for you and read them through?' she offered contritely, taking up the roll from the West Indies. 'I could let you know if there is any definite news and spare you the admonishments.'

'Please do,' said Marianne with a grimace.

The door burst open, and Laura in a most elegant wrapper of striped blue gauze over a white glazed-cotton lining, came in with a flushed face. 'How dare you?' she demanded of Alice.

'How dare I what?' asked Alice, while her mind scurried over the various misdemeanours she and Marianne had been committing.

'Sir Geoffrey is furious!' hissed Laura. 'I have never seen him so angry before in my life!'

'Laura, please tell me what you are talking about,' said Alice while Marianne watched, a most interested observer, from her bed. 'I have no idea why Geoffrey should be so angry with me.'

'You are taking him to law about Sir Walter's will. You—you—you shameless hussy!' cried Laura in the highest indignation. 'How can you be so ungrateful? When we have sheltered you and fed you all this time and taken you into society as though nothing had happened.'

'I am sorry to offend you, Laura, but you must see that I have to look after my own interests,' said Alice, at last understanding the outburst, and trying to hide a sinking dread.

'Dragging your mother's disgrace into the light of day—publishing it on the very front pages of the newspapers!' cried Laura. 'Does not your womanly heart shrink from such exposure?'

'As to that,' said Alice coldly. 'You made quite sure that all our acquaintance knew every detail of my

141

mother's disgrace within hours of learning it yourself. Why should it be so much worse for the world at large to know?'

'Lost to all decent feeling!' cried Laura, sinking into a chair and wringing her hands.

'May I offer you a cup of tea?' asked Marianne solicitously.

'I should have thrown you out of the house,' cried Laura, 'for the nameless trollop that you are.'

'Laura!' cried Alice, appalled at the language and the vicious tone.

'If Alice's lawyers get their way, dear Lady Lacey,' said Marianne sweetly, 'she may be nameless, but she certainly will not be a trollop, and you will be unable to throw her out of this house for it will belong to her, not you.'

'Oh!' Laura's exasperation rose in a scream and she buried her face in her hands.

'My brother must be furious,' Alice said rapidly and quietly to Marianne over Laura's head. 'I think we should pack our clothes and prepare to take refuge with the Gormans.'

'No. Wait. We need advice from Mr Christopher. What I said was true. I suspect that this still is your house, and it will be much easier to get them out while we are still here than to try and dislodge them if you win your case.'

'I couldn't *bear* much more of this,' said Alice distastefully, looking down at Laura who had dissolved into noisy sobs.

There was a tap at the door and the page put his head round to ask if Miss Alice could spare a few moments in the study with Sir Geoffrey. Marianne's eyes met those of Alice. It was a strangely polite message for a man who was about to quarrel violently with his sister.

'You must go,' Marianne whispered. 'Are you frightened? Do you want me to come with you?'

'No. I am not frightened of Geoffrey,' Alice replied

142

quietly. She sent word that she would attend her brother as soon as she was dressed. Marianne reminded her to put on riding clothes as they were expected in the park. 'If you are delayed, I may have to leave without you,' she whispered, and then bent over Lady Lacey solicitously.

'You sent for me, Geoffrey,' Alice said some twenty minutes later. Her head was held high. The long slim lines of the dark blue riding skirt gave her added height and her brother thought he had never seen her looking so stately and dignified.

'Mr Sellop tells me that you propose to take me to court for the restoration of your inheritance. You must be mad. I cannot believe it.'

'It is true,' Alice replied calmly.

'How could you have contrived such an underhanded scheme behind my back—and when you were sheltering under my roof—nay, feeding from my hand?' asked the baronet in righteous indignation. 'This must stop. You must order your lawyer to bring the whole thing to a close. It is a persecution.'

'The fact that you were living under my roof and permitting me to feed yourself, Laura and Clara did not prevent you taking underhanded action against me earlier this year,' said Alice. 'I believe you were at work three months or more before I heard of it.'

'That has nothing to do with the case,' Geoffrey said hotly. 'A gross injustice had been done due to the partiality of my father, and it was only proper that it should be righted.' His fingers started picking at the frayed edges of a big leather-bound book that lay on the desk.

'As to that,' Alice responded, 'the gross injustice may lie in what you are doing now. There is no doubt in anybody's mind where my father wished to leave the Lacey money. Your claim to it only lies on a legal quibble over a name. My father's intent was clear, and

143

if people are to be allowed to will their money as they wish, then justice is on my side, my dear brother, and not upon yours.'

'Father must have been out of his mind to leave the Lacey property to a woman.' Geoffrey turned away from her to hide his rising irritability. He had always hated being crossed. 'If he had left the disposition of the property to me, this would never have happened.'

'Naturally,' said Alice drily. As Geoffrey paced in front of the window, she could see that the last few weeks. of increased prosperity had not improved his appearance. He had always had a surface manner of respectable calm, but now smouldering fircs were threatening to break through. Under strain, as now, his face became flushed and a vein throbbed on his forehead. He had been a much happier man, Alice guessed, when things had been as they were before.

'Family squabbles in front of a judge with reporters from the newspapers scribbling away are unthinkable,' he said. 'Every sordid detail of my father's life would be dragged out into the open and served up to the public for them to scorn. It would be bad enough for me, but for you, Alice, it would be the end of all future prospects. Your name would become a bye-word. No-one would receive you. You would be the subject of scorn. And for what purpose? You can get nothing from the will as your name is not Alice Lacey. You are throwing away your money on costs and dragging your reputation in the mud. Be reasonable. Instruct your attorney to stop the proceedings. Then, when you have accepted the fact that the will must be set aside, we can reach some form of agreement . . .'

'Father's will is *not* to be set aside,' Alice said firmly. Though her brother's voice had risen during his speech, she was not to be browbeaten.

'Alice you must listen to me!' he commanded her angrily. 'Mr Sellop says that you have no case at all.'

'Then it need not annoy you, Geoffrey,' she said.

144

'It does not annoy me!' he cried, pulling at the cloth around his neck. 'It merely creates difficulties where there need be none.'

'Let us agree,' said Alice gently, for his colour was rising, 'to leave the question entirely to the lawyers. If you are so sure of the rights of your side, this will not be difficult for you and it will leave me some small hope to live by. Geoffrey,' she begged, for she saw that she had only angered him further, 'we have managed to live as brother and sister until now. Don't give the world the pleasure of seeing us fight like savages.'

'Savages!' cried her brother, much offended. 'You had better talk of wild animals, as I have been nurturing a viper in my breast.'

Alice could not repress a smile.

'You think you're so clever!' thundered Sir Geoffrey, and old nursery rivalries came bubbling to the surface. He glared at his beautiful sister, always so quick, so capable, so beloved of their papa. 'Get out,' he shouted. 'Get out of my house. Get out of my life. Take your nasty legal pettifoggery elsewhere!' He came across the room and seized her by the shoulders. Daisy Stebbings' eyes glared under her son's eyebrows in impotent fury. Geoffrey stared through Alice. What was it that made these others so much more intelligent, so deeply beloved? When the real value of things and people could only be judged by money. 'Who is paying for all this, anyway?' he demanded.

Alice was dumb.

He shook her hard. 'I require you to tell me who is financing you. By God, I command you, Alice. The costs will be enormous.'

'Please let me go, Geoffrey,' said Alice coldly.

He dropped his hands. 'Sorry,' he mumbled, groping his way back to the desk. 'Sit down. I apologize. I shouldn't have sworn in front of you—but things— Laura—difficulty . . .' he muttered uneasily. Alice began

145

to feel alarmed. The Geoffrey she had known in former days would not have broken down like this.

'I suppose some beggarly barrister is taking the case on speculation, eh?' he burst out again. 'Stir up as much dirt as he can and then split the profits with you. That's it, isn't it? Well, I won't have it, d'ye hear, Alice? Who are you to set yourself against me? A nameless, penniless nonentity!' He hammered on the desk and the blood rose to his head and made him gasp.

'Calm yourself, Geoffrey,' cried Alice sharply, 'or you'll bring on a seizure.'

He had begun to choke. She ran to his side and disregarding the hands that tried to push her off, unfastened his neckcloth and his collar. He gulped in air and then sank forward with his head on his arms.

Alice ran to a cupboard in the wall and came back with a small glass of brandy. 'Drink this,' she said, laying her hand on his arm, and he raised bloodshot eyes and drank.

'I'm sorry if I went too far, Alice,' he mumbled.

'Do not think of it,' she said. 'You were beyond yourself. I will fetch Laura.'

'No—wait—we haven't settled anything yet. You must leave this house. You can see that it would be impossible for you to remain here if we are going to fight in court.'

'I do not see ...'

'I will provide for you,' he offered, peering up into her face. 'I will find some respectable house, perhaps a cottage at Holt Lacey ...'

'No,' said Alice with decision. 'I will not leave London until the case has been decided.'

He rose rather unsteadily 'Then you force me to act as I had hoped not to do. I command you to get your things together and go from my home.'

'It may not be your home, Geoffrey.'

'What?' The corner of his mouth had started to twitch.

'If the lawyers succeed in having father's will maintained,' Alice said, mentally blessing Marianne's quick wits, 'this house has never ceased to be mine. I could as well command you to leave it.'

He snarled at her. There was no other way to describe the quick drawback of his narrow lips from his teeth. 'I'll see you in hell first,' he said.

She drew her breath. This was not her staid brother. What was happening to Geoffrey? 'I will fetch Laura,' she said and hurried from the room.

It seemed that Marianne and Clara had already left for the park, and Marianne had left a message that Alice was to hurry after. An under-groom was walking Alice's roan horse in front of the house and would go with her and stay until she had joined the two other girls.

After Alice had found Laura, and told her that Geoffrey was a little unwell, she mounted and moved off mechanically. The late scene had shaken her deeply. Through all the unpleasant things that had happened to her, Alice had believed that her brother was activated by a dogged sense of what was right—glad enough to increase his wealth, but guided by proper principle. Now she had glimpsed emotions that she had not known were there—a jealous hatred and a wish to grind her down. It was as though he had resented her from the cradle and wanted her wealth with unnatural craving. However much he might harm Alice, he was certainly doing himself no good. She shivered.

'There's Miss Brown,' said the groom at her side, and she perceived Clara in the distance on the edge of a great concourse of carriages and riders which included many of their friends. Alice trotted towards them and the groom went home. Where was her cousin? She edged her mount to the deep shade of some elm trees, for she had started trembling again. Was it safe to continue living in Portman Square? Another time Geoffrey might not stop at shaking her.

A well-known laugh made her turn round swiftly. She had not been the only rider that morning to seek a little

147

privacy. Marianne and Matthew were also sheltering under the concealing arms of the elms, and their horses were standing nose to tail while the riders were engrossed in conversation. How well Mr Vale sat on his horse! Animal and man were well matched. Each was tall and each, one felt, kept great strength easily under control beneath their glossy black coats! Alice's heart gave an unmaidenly lurch in her bosom. Then Matthew Vale laughed aloud and briefly put his hand over Marianne's. Alice froze. Whatever her brother might do, it could not cause the pang that now smote her. Geoffrey's hatred was nothing to Matthew Vale's indifference. If he were to become the husband of Marianne, then Alice did not care who was the chief inheritor of the Lacey fortune. She recognized her true wishes and Matthew Vale was at the centre of them all.

'Alice!' called Marianne gaily, and the two riders came over to where she was. 'You are still alive! I thought Geoffrey would have eaten you. Tell me, was it dreadful? Are we to be thrown out on our ears?'

'It was a very unpleasant experience,' Alice admitted.

'Whoops! Tally-ho!' cried Captain Wargate, galloping up in a disgracefully rowdy manner. 'There's Miss St George! This is the horse I was telling you about. Come and watch me put him through his paces.'

'Mr Vale will tell you what has been arranged,' said Marianne hastily, 'but I must join Clara or there will be a scandal,' and with a grimace in their direction, she guided her horse into the open.

'You are not looking well,' Matthew told Alice. 'Is your brother tyrannizing over you? Would it not be better to leave his protection until things are smooth again?'

'Yes . . . no. That is, perhaps you are right,' said Alice, barely knowing what she was saying. 'Geoffrey —I—it was frightening to find how much he *hates* me, Mr Vale. I must have been really high-handed towards him and Laura when I was—before this trouble came.

I didn't know I was behaving badly, but they must have felt it or they wouldn't loathe me so much now.'

'Not at all,' he said, leaning over to take her rein and gently encouraging their horses to follow Marianne. 'That is not the case. The fact that you were generous to them before actually makes them behave worse to you at present.'

'How so?'

'It irritates them. It causes them uncomfortable feelings inside which they have to take out on you. If you had been proud and demanding and ordered them about before, they would be treating you with much more forbearance at this moment.'

'But that is not logical,' objected Alice.

Mr Vale laughed. 'Not at all logical,' he agreed, 'but nevertheless quite true.'

'Well it is quite right that Geoffrey should feel uncomfortable,' said Alice, 'because my mother was so very kind to him when he was young.'

'If your mother is vindicated,' said Matthew, 'I trust he will feel a great deal worse,' and he turned to talk to one of his many friends in the group that they had now joined.

'He is ready enough to take Marianne aside to exchange confidences,' Alice thought miserably. It did not occur to her that Mr Vale was careful to guard her own reputation as something much more precious than that of the heiress from St Kitts.

CHAPTER THIRTEEN

'Laura, you must persuade Alice that it is in her interest to leave this house,' Geoffrey told his wife. He had been cosseted and comforted and given some more brandy, and he had returned to his normal self-esteem. 'How she can wish to stay under our roof when she is openly quarrelling with us in court, I cannot understand.'

'No, Geoffrey.'

'I seem to have lost all influence over her,' he admitted, 'especially since her cousin came to stay.'

'Oh yes, my love, it is wicked the way that Alice disregards your wishes.'

'And towards this Miss St George,' said Geoffrey, 'I have no duty whatsoever. She is not a Lacey relative. She has no claim on us at all. And her coming when she did was most unfortunate. Alice seemed to be accepting her true position quite becomingly before the other girl arrived.'

'Very true.'

'We must make it clear to Miss St George that her presence here is no longer welcome. You must speak to her, Laura. Tell her so tonight. She must make other arrangements to stay in London or she must go back to where she came from. When Alice is on her own again,' estimated Sir Geoffrey, 'she will soon come round to seeing things in their proper proportion.'

Laura was thinking very fast. Marianne's 'assistance' for the previous month had already gone a long way towards silencing the most demanding of the tradesmen, and if she were to be bundled out of the house before the next lot of bills were due it would, Laura felt, be most unfortunate timing. And what about the forthcoming Lacey ball? Laura had spared no cost in its arrangement, for Marianne was to pay for it all. And it was far too late to think of cancelling it. Nearly everyone had accepted, and it stood fair to being one of the highlights of the Season. The Prime Minister said he might drop in! Laura's heart quailed within her as she remembered all the salmon she had ordered which was coming by midnight train from the west of Scotland . . .

'There is one thing, Geoffrey . . .' she hazarded.

'What is it?' he asked in irritation. Amendments from his wife were no more welcome than from his sister.

'It is about Percy. It is rather delicate.'

'Well?'

'You see, my dearest, Miss St George and Percy have quarrelled.'

'And what is that to me?'

'Well—people do not fall out with people unless they have been a little intimate before. Now Percy makes no secret of his feelings, but I have never been sure how Miss St George looked upon him. But last night at the party she would not speak to Percy. Every time he came to our side of the room, she tilted her nose and walked away.'

'Miss St George can do what she likes with her nose, Laura, and it is no concern of mine.'

'Then, just as we were leaving, she gave him a little look over her shoulder. I am sure it was meant to be forgiving. He hadn't touched his supper. He looked quite distraught.'

'My dear Laura, I am not interested in their looks or their suppers.'

'No, but Geoffrey I would prefer to have Miss St George under my eye at this most interesting period. It would be such a wonderful catch for Percy. He could give up the law altogether and concentrate on his parliamentary career.'

But to her chagrin Laura found that such an argument had no influence on Sir Geoffrey whatever. 'As to your brother, he must take his chances with the rest of them,' he said. 'And I am bound to declare that I feel

Miss St George could do much better for herself than Percy Brown.'

'It is not only Marianne,' said Laura, 'but Alice. Have you not noticed how very particular Mr Bunne has become in his attentions?'

'Bunne?' asked the baronet. 'That pious conservative? He'll be getting himself a bad name, they tell me, if he pursues his actions on behalf of fallen women much further.'

'Of course he will drop all that when he is married to Alice,' Laura said.

'Has he actually offered?' demanded Geoffrey.

'Not in so many words, my love, but it can only be a matter of days. In fact tonight at the concert I will make it my business to bring them together, and he can hardly fail to make a declaration. Only think what a pity it would be if we turned Alice away at this juncture and frightened Mr Bunne off.'

'Bunne,' said Sir Geoffrey thoughtfully. 'Yes—Bunne's a sensible man. He would soon come to terms with this case and persuade Alice to drop all her pretensions. I wouldn't mind dealing with Bunne.'

'A truly moral character,' agreed Laura.

'You are right. Bunne's the last man to want to profit out of her mother's infamous behaviour. He would look upon it as the wages of sin. So Bunne's the man, is he? It couldn't be better,' said Sir Geoffrey, becoming a great deal more cheerful.

'And Alice may stay here a little while longer?' asked Laura.

'Yes. Very well. As you say, it would be a pity to lose such a chance by being overhasty.'

'Do not mention Mr Bunne to Alice,' warned Laura. 'You know how headstrong she is. She might take against him.'

'Alice has got too much good sense to turn down so respectable an offer,' said Geoffrey. 'Bunne! I could not be better pleased.'

After their ride, Marianne and Alice slipped into the house and upstairs as quietly as they could, leaving Clara to flounce into the drawing-room and demand an iced drink before changing.

'I wonder what Geoffrey has decided,' Alice said to her cousin when she joined her in her bedroom after putting on a simple morning frock of cherry-flowered cotton. Its starched folds hung stiffly over her crinoline without the need for petticoats—a distinct advantage on a day so hot as this. 'We should be prepared, Marianne, to be thrown out on the streets at any moment.'

'Well we could go to a hotel if the worst came to the worst. What is it, Phoebe?'

Phoebe was understood to say that Josephus was now feeling a little better and anxious to speak to Miss Alice.

'To Miss Marianne,' corrected Alice, but Phoebe shook her head.

'Mistress Euphemie done send this man for see about Miss Alice business,' she assured them.

'Then bring him here by all means,' said Marianne. 'No. Wait. It would be more suitable to bring him to the drawing-room. Do that, please, Phoebe . . . now where are those letters? You promised you would read them to me. Come to the drawing-room Alice—but sit here, away from the windows, I beg you. I shall have to give up riding. I cannot understand how the London ladies can expose themselves so rashly to the sun. I am getting as brown as a nut! Only look at my hands—I shall have to keep them hidden when I go back to St Kitts or I would not dare visit my friends again. They would think I had been employed as a farm labourer. Is anything the matter, Alice? You have gone quite pale.'

'Marianne,' said Alice in a strange voice, 'there are not only letters here. Aunt Euphemie has sent a book as well—look!'

'What sort of book?'

'A poetry book.'

'Strange . . . my aunt is not much in favour of poetry.'

'But look—on the fly leaf,' cried Alice. 'It is inscribed by my mother . . .' and she showed the front page of a slim little volume bound in soft leather which was mildewed from tropical humidity.

Given to me by my dear husband Walter Lacey on the day of our marriage.

> Amelie Lestrange Lacey
> Frenchman's Point, Nevis.

The thin old spiky handwriting was in faded brown ink, and the rest of the page had been torn away.

'Alice! So they were married! It is all a lie,' cried Marianne joyfully. 'Oh wait until we show this to Geoffrey,' she exalted. 'I cannot wait to see Laura's face! And Clara's. How angry they will be!'

Silent tears were running down Alice's cheeks. Deep feelings of thankfulness that her mother had not been the wanton woman she was painted moved her more than she could say.

'But I do not know how Aunt Euphemie knew about it all so quickly,' said Marianne, picking up the papers and scanning them with rapid eyes. 'Ah! Yes of course! When she wrote this she had not yet heard from me.'

'Then how?'

'You wrote to me, apparently, telling me not to come here this Season as soon as you knew that there was trouble.'

'That is true, although I had forgotten it.'

'Aunt Euphemie received the letter after I had left, and she opened it to see if she should send it back to London. When she read what had happened to you, she was enraged—*L'honneur de la famille,* you know—and hastened to find any scrap of evidence she could lay hands upon about dear Aunt Amelie's wedding. Wait!' Marianne read on. 'Oh Alice!'

'What is it?'

'That man—Josephus—Aunt Euphemie says he was

155

your mother's house-steward and *actually present at your mother's wedding!*'

'Thank God!' said Alice profoundly. Tears kept pouring down. She had not known how great a strain the last few weeks had been. Now it was all to be washed away—the shock, the shame and the daily humiliation. Now her future was as secure and bright as it had ever been before this nightmare had descended. Now she could think once more of Matthew Vale— *or could she?* Had his affection been lost?

'Here the old man,' said Phoebe, ushering in the person whose presence had suddenly become so vital.

'Josephus!' cried Alice through her tears. 'You were my dear mother's steward?'

He took her hand lovingly and a wide smile lit up his face. 'I born Mistress Amelie plantation and be her slave long time before she make me free. She teach me write my name, and do accounts and many things.'

'Oh Josephus,' cried Alice. 'We need you so badly. Will you help me?'

'I very glad help you, Mistress. You very like Mistress Amelie, same face for her exactly.'

'Tell me then, do you remember when she married?'

'I do, Mistress.'

'And you remember my father? The man she was married to? Sir Walter Lacey?'

'I remember the young master, Mistress. Came from England on the ship.'

'Yes. Yes. Oh I am so happy that you remember. Where did the marriage take place?'

'Mistress?'

'The actual nuptial ceremony. Was it in a place of worship?'

Josephus' face was quite blank.

'Go on, you fool old man,' Phoebe prompted him without malice. 'You tell Miss Alice what place you go see she mama marry this sir from England.'

It took a great deal of help from Phoebe and a great

deal of puzzlement on the part of Josephus to establish that the marriage had taken place in the small Catholic chapel on Nevis, that it had been in the dead of night, and that nobody had been present but the priest and his clerk, the bridal pair and Josephus.

'But was it *legal?*' asked Alice. 'Did they enter the marriage in the book? Was there *writing?*' Alice persisted.

'I write my name. Englishman gave me five guineas,' Josephus remembered vividly.

'Thank God,' murmered Alice again. Then, 'Josephus, after the marriage my mother went to England, did she not?'

'Mistress?'

'Miss Amelie she go for England with that Englishman,' Phoebe prompted.

Josephus nodded. 'For true,' he said. 'Mistress Amelie done send me to St Kitts. Make me promise I never say nothing to nobody about she marrying.' He shook his head. 'But Mistress Euphemie say I tell you now about it and show the locket.'

'Locket?' asked Alice. 'What does he mean?'

'Wait a minute,' said Marianne. 'There is something about a locket in Aunt Euphemie's letter—here! "Josephus has a relic of my dear cousin's which I cannot get him to part with. Therefore he has to come." '

Alice turned back to the old man. 'Josephus, what is this locket? Please let me see.'

He hesitated noticeably. 'Dat thing belong for me,' he said.

'Yes. I know. I don't want to take it from you. Just let me see it.'

'Mistress Amelie done give it me.'

'Yes. We know. It's yours. No-one is going to steal it from you. Just let me see.'

'Mistress Amelie make me swear. Make I never show any other person. Never. So strike me dead.'

'Oooooh, you wicked bad creature!' cried Phoebe,

157

giving his arm a shake. 'How dare you stop from what the Mistress tell you do, then? Go on, you naughty thing, you.'

Alice stepped forward to intervene, for the old man was very frail, but Phoebe seemed to have triggered off the desired effect. From the front of his shirt, with many doubtful mutterings and hesitations, Josephus' old hand drew forth first a thin gold chain, then a slim gold locket with a diamond mounted at the centre.

'Ayeeeee! You wicked thing! You go for steal your mistress' jewel!' cried Phoebe, greatly shocked.

'I never so!' Josephus was filled with great indignation. 'Mistress done give me that with her own hand.'

'Be quiet, Phoebe,' cried Marianne. 'Look, Alice.'

The two girls came close. There was no hope of detaching the small relic from the old man. They were able to hold the locket, but he clung on grimly to the chain about his neck.

With careful excited fingers Alice pressed the diamond, then the gold knobs at the edge of the locket, trying to find the spring. At last it came softly open. The inside held two similar oval frames, each containing a tiny portrait.

'*Tante Amelie*!' whispered Marianne. 'How extraordinarily you resemble her, Alice.'

'My father! But so much younger than when I knew him.' They looked, then looked at each other, and then the back of the case. 'Walter–Amelie,' Alice read tenderly.

Marianne sniffed. 'All my life I have thought of Aunt Amelie as a saint,' she said, 'and to come here and find Geoffrey maligning her, hurt me more than I can express.'

'Marianne!' said Alice. 'Are these things *proof*? Is a locket and an inscription in a book of poems enough to convince a judge that a marriage has taken place?'

'I don't know. I don't think so! One needs a witness?'

'If the judge knows anything about the Colonies,' said

158

Marianne candidly, 'he would know that for fifty pounds anyone could buy a dozen witnesses. Where are those letters again? Aunt Euphemie may say something else.'

Marianne sat down in her chair to study more closely what her great-aunt had written. Alice took up the locket again with reverent fingers and looked at the twining, florid inscription once more. 'Walter–Amelie . . .' she repeated, 'and these curls are a date—1828. My dearest papa looks different without his beard and whiskers. Not much like Geoffrey though. He favours the other side.'

'Aunt Euphemie says,' remarked Marianne, 'that she is certain that she can find legal confirmation that a marriage took place on Nevis. "Meanwhile," she says, "I am sending you Josephus and his locket as a sop to keep the attorneys busy and to maintain Alice in her proper station. That her base-born brother should seek to sully the fair name of a St George descendant is something which I will never forgive." Well!' said Marianne. 'I didn't know Great-Aunt Euphemie had so much fight left in her! Why does she call Geoffrey base-born, Alice? Was his mother altogether low?'

'Not at all. Her father was in trade, which was a great stigma in those days I believe, but the family was perfectly respectable,' said Alice. 'Aunt Euphemie has old-fashioned ideas.'

'She is actually going over to Nevis herself!' cried Marianne, coming to the end of the long sheets of the letter. 'How strange! She hasn't left Beauregarde for fifteen years or more. Great heavens—I wish I were there to see it! They have chartered a scow from San Eustatius with a litter on deck that sways against the movement of the sea. It will be like an ancient promenade of Queen Elizabeth!'

'How kind of your aunt to go to all this trouble for me,' said Alice.

'I expect she is having the time of her life,' said

159

Marianne. 'Well, Alice, what are we to do? The first thing, I suppose, is to get the evidence to Mr Christopher. Josephus—you give me that locket I send for lawyer man, after he give back to you.'

'No, mistress. Never. This thing stay for me. I done promise Mistress Amelie upon my life.'

'Oh please, Josephus,' begged Alice. 'It is only for a short while. Do let us borrow it. It shall be given back to you.'

'No, Mistress Alice. I done swear.'

'Go away, you old man, you,' cried Phoebe. 'Do as the Mistress tell you. What sort of fellow you think you are, then, go say no, no, when Mistress command you do some thing.'

The old man's eyes filled with tears, but in spite of that Alice would have persisted gently until she got her way. It was Marianne who said sharply, 'Leave him alone, Phoebe. He is not to be pushed. No-one shall make him break his word. If we can't get the locket to the lawyer, Alice, we must get the lawyer to the locket. How can we manage it?'

'Oh Marianne, it may be needed *in court*.' Alice fingered the locket lovingly. 'Walter–Amelie, 1828,' she read, closed it and laid it down. 'With Josephus as witness that *must* be evidence,' she said.

'I am sure it is. And if necessary Josephus shall show it in the court. But I am not going to have my servants forced to go against their sworn obligations—why, what is the matter, Alice?' For Alice had let out a sudden dismayed cry.

'It cannot be evidence! For it is not true.'

'What do you mean?'

'1828!' cried Alice. 'My parents were married in 1840. This *wasn't* a wedding remembrance! 1828 must have been the year in which my father first went to Nevis, when they were betrothed. But he came back to England then and married Geoffrey's mother and left my mama to eat her heart out for him on her plantation.'

160

'Just a betrothal gift,' said Marianne sadly. 'And the book of poems must have come later. What a shame! Still, we should show it to Mr Christopher. And we still have Josephus' word.'

'I don't think the word of a black slave would be believed in an English court,' said an angry voice unexpectedly. 'Even if you could understand what he said. And I heard about the five guineas—he was bribed!' And Clara came forward from the far end of the room where she had been hidden by the long curtains.

'Clara! You have no business to listen to private conversations. It is unforgivable!' cried Alice, aghast.

'And you've no right to bring nasty paid informers into my sister's house,' retorted the young girl as she flounced out.

'She will tell Laura!' cried Alice in dismay.

'*Tant pis!*' shrugged Marianne. 'With any luck, Laura will not be here much longer to bother us, my dear Alice.'

Alice fell silent. So near . . . and yet so far. One moment's hope seemed to follow another's despair with fateful persistence. For a moment she was tempted to cut through the whole knot, give up and disappear to a cottage on the Holt Lacey estate as her brother desired.

Then she stiffened herself. It was a question of her mother's reputation. She gave herself a little shake. 'Phoebe,' she said. 'You should take Josephus to lie down now. He is not looking well. How do you feel, Josephus? Was the voyage a great strain on you?'

'I think I suffer small swamp sickness, Mistress,' he agreed.

'Get the silver flask of rum from my travelling-case, Phoebe,' said Marianne, 'and mix a little with some lime juice—no, you do not have limes here, do you, Alice? What a pity. Then ask the housekeeper for a lemon, Phoebe, and squeeze the juice into a thin glass with two measures of rum. Put a silver spoon in the

161

glass and pour on a single measure of boiling water. Do you understand?'

'For sure, Miss Marianne.'

'Then wrap Josephus tight in woollen blankets and let him sweat the sickness out. He will feel fresh as a lark in the morning.'

CHAPTER FOURTEEN

'I do not despise rum for medicinal purposes,' Marianne explained to Alice. 'Only in excess, when it turns a gentleman into a soak. And I wonder whether a lemon has the same properties as a lime? Perhaps I should have told Phoebe to use two.'

'She will be lucky to find one, the whole house is in such an upset. The area steps are covered with barrels, there are cases of straw and glass all over the hall, and Laura has had the covers taken off the chairs almost at the very last moment.'

'There is always a fuss in a house before a ball.'

'Not like this. I have been amazed. She should have set things in motion as soon as the invitations went out.'

Two footmen came into the drawing-room. 'That's Miss St George,' the one explained to the other. 'You bow and offer the salver and say, "A letter, please, Miss".'

The younger one did as he was told, only he went to Alice. 'A letter, please, Miss Lacey,' he said carefully.

'Miss!' thundered the outraged footman. 'And not that Miss, the other one. He'll never learn if he lives to be a hundred,' he explained to Alice apologetically. 'He's had that letter by him all day, thinking it was for Lady Lacey. And I can't get him properly trained, things being as they are.'

'That will do nicely thank you, John,' Alice told him. 'And you are quite right to stay at his side until he has learnt his job. You can leave now.'

'Well, well, well, well, well,' said Marianne, who had opened her letter. 'So much for your excessive caution, Alice. I did not think perfect gentlemen wrote notes to perfect ladies.'

'There is no such thing as a perfect gentleman,' said

Alice seriously, 'but we can help to keep them up to standard. Who is writing to you now?'

'Mr Percy Brown.'

'You surprise me.'

'Not so much as I have been surprised. Listen to this—

"My dear Miss St George,
   Your words have wounded me. I never before considered, fool that I was, how desperate is the plight of young ladies like yourself on whom the full glare of the world is turned with all its inclination to suspicion, but who have yet no masculine relation to lift the weight of practical business from off their shoulders."

What a sentence, Alice! It is impossible to read in one breath. Still, an apology is always welcome, especially if one has not earned it. Let us see if there is any juice in all this cane—

"But sympathy and understanding are not enough, and I wish to show practical help. I have been to see your attorney, Mr Christopher, and arranged that he shall visit Mrs Gorman in Cavendish Square this afternoon. I hope this will be convenient for you? I know Miss Alice will need no excuse for calling on her godmother.
                                Yours very sincerely,
                                Percy Brown."

'Well!' cried Marianne. 'Whoever would have thought it of him? Not only to acknowledge himself wrong, but actually to do something positive about it. There is more to Mr Percy Brown than I had thought.'

'I must say I am surprised. It verges on deception. He would never have behaved like that two months ago. You have had a marked influence on him, Marianne.'

'And did he need it! This has been the first time he has behaved like anything but a clucking wet-nurse since I arrived. In sixty years he might become quite a man of decision.'

'Well I wish he had not picked on my godmother's house for the rendezvous,' said Alice. 'For Violet

Gorman is still awaiting her delivery, and I know this is causing dismay. I would not like to bring her further trouble.'

'We will go and come quickly,' said Marianne. 'But I must have food first, because I am quite starved. Why is the house so quiet?'

'Laura and Clara are taking lunch with friends.'

'Then let us have our lunch and I will order the carriage to be here at a quarter after three. Can you reach the bell for me, Alice? Or shall we walk? It is only a stone's throw, after all.'

The Gorman house in Cavendish Square was ominously quiet. A silent butler led Alice and Marianne on tiptoe into a drawing-room with the blinds half drawn. In the shadows stood the tall figure of a man in dark clothing, and Alice bowed to him nervously. Marianne went close and sank into a respectful bob. 'Good afternoon, Father,' she said, modestly dropping her head.

'Are you of the faith, my child?' he enquired, coming forward and revealing long, grey, stern, ascetic features.

'No, Father, but the main stem of my family is. My Great-Aunt Angelique entered the Convent of Poor Clares on Martinique and was there for more than twenty years.'

'Oh Miss, it is so good to see you!' cried a young voice, and Mary pattered in and curtsyed eagerly. 'And Miss St George! Oh Miss, you've got your hair all different—who does that for you now?'

'My cousin's maid,' laughed Alice. 'I am glad to see you, Mary. Are you happy here with Mrs Gorman?'

'Ever so happy, Miss. Madam's an easy lady once you get to know her.' Mary paused and cocked an anxious ear. 'And I get two pounds a quarter extra, Miss, for starching the altar cloths at the oratory. They says they've never been brought up so nice before—was that a scream, Miss?'

'No. I didn't hear anything. Did you, Marianne?'

'And Miss—one of the grooms is interested. He comes from down our way and he's as steady a man as you would wish to meet.'

'Oh Mary, I am so happy for you.'

'Yes, Miss. Only I can't do anything about it till I've seen my mother, because it means changing my church,' and she dropped a curtsy in the direction of the priest. 'Oooh! wasn't that a call?' she asked, looking over her shoulder.

'What's the matter, Mary?' asked Alice.

'It's the midwife,' hissed the little maid, dropping her voice so that the gentleman could not possibly hear. 'Being called during the night, she had to keep her strength up on porter.'

'Has young Mrs Gorman reached her time at last?' asked Alice. 'We must leave. They would not welcome our presence now.'

'No, wait,' interrupted Marianne quickly. 'Mary, a young man is to come here—a Mr Christopher. We only want a few words with him and then we can go without disturbing the family.'

'No amorous dalliance shall take place in my presence,' proclaimed a hollow voice from the background.

'Dear Father,' said Marianne, whirling round upon him. 'This is no lovers' tryst, I promise you. My cousin —Miss Alice, here—has been most grossly used by her cruel brother, and this is the only—why, what was that?'

The shuttered peace split with an explosion of breaking china. A door slammed. Footsteps hurried, and there was a huge angry bellow of female rage.

'Get below stairs you thankless slut and put your head into a bucket of cold water!' cried the stentorian voice of the elder Mrs Gorman. 'And if you leave it there, it will be the best day's work you have done for many years. Your pardon, Father,' she added in parenthesis, as Marianne, Alice, Mary and the priest rushed out into

166

the hall. 'And if you dare set foot in my daughter-in-law's room again, I will have you clapped in Newgate, do you hear?'

A broken wash-basin lay in small pieces on the marble-flagged floor and a jug of water sailed down to join it and to splash the audience with drops and chips.

'Aaaaaaaar!' a huge roar of rage came from a fat, filthy figure of a woman with wild red hair who was clinging to the bannisters at the top of the stairs and shaking a mottled arm in Mrs Gorman's general direction. 'Below stairs, is it?' she cried. 'Not wanting me now? And me all the way up from Deptford to look after the poor little thing. I won't stand for it. Let me through!' and she launched herself into Mrs Gorman's impressive figure, though not quite upon the direct line.

'Unhand me!' thundered the dowager, putting out strong arms to defend herself.

'Get out of me way!' screamed the other at the top of her voice. 'I'm coming! Can ye hear me, my little darling? Sure it's a fine boy just waiting for Catherine O'Malley to bring into the world thish day—ay—ay.' Her voice rose beyond hearing, as the scuffle between herself and Mrs Gorman ended. 'God shave me!' she cried, tottering at the top of the stairs, 'for a poor, afflicted innocent, peace-loving . . .' and describing an untidy arc, she fell and rolled to the bottom of the staircase, where she opened blue eyes, looked at the priest, said, 'Forgive me, Father, for I have sinned,' hiccoughed, closed her eyes and started to snore.

'Great heavens!' cried Alice in horror. 'She is dead.'

'As drunk as a lord,' corrected Marianne, and she called upwards. 'We must apologize for visiting you at an awkward time, Mrs Gorman.'

The dowager showed signs of bursting asunder with rage and desperation as she came downstairs and stepped over the prostrate woman without a glance. 'Scum of the earth!' she pronounced in tones that made Alice jump.

167

'She is the mother of fourteen, six living,' came the hollow voice again, 'and she never misses mass except for reasons of health.'

Mrs Gorman threw up her hands, but she was not going to argue with her spiritual adviser. 'I am at my wit's end,' she proclaimed. 'I do not know which way to turn. The housekeeper is in her room with cotton in her ears, John is trying to console Violet when it is not fit for him to remain in the room any longer, and Catherine O'Malley who had the highest references—oh, Father, you must help me. There must be one decent midwife in your congregation. I interviewed seventeen, but they all stank of gin.'

A door opened above and John Gorman leaned over the bannisters. 'Violet needs help, Mother,' he cried. 'Where is a woman? The doctor cannot manage alone.' He was dishevelled and distressed and Alice felt deep pangs of sympathy. But what could she do? She was totally ignorant and did not know any way to help.

'My maid, Phoebe, has very great experience,' said Marianne promptly. 'She is always summoned to these events at Beauregarde.'

'Where is she?' asked Mrs Gorman, looking all about her.

'In Portman Square. I will fetch her immediately,' said Marianne, and she was across the hall and through the door in a moment. Then Alice realized that Mr Christopher had entered and was standing politely at the drawing-room door.

'Come, Father, you may be needed,' said Mrs Gorman turning to the stairs again, 'and you,' she shook her finger at Mr Christopher, 'stay where you are, young man. He may need another bag.' With which cryptic instruction she disappeared along the landing.

'Let us go into the drawing-room,' said Alice, for two servants had appeared to help Mary carry the drunken midwife from view. 'There is so much that I wish to tell you, if only I can get my senses in order again.'

168

'Before you begin, I should explain that your hope was quite unfounded.'

'My hope?'

'Yes. Of a shipboard marriage. I have checked, and none took place.'

'Oh that! I had forgotten it. Such a lot has happened since then, and before I forget, my brother hinted this morning that he would give me some provision if I dropped the case against him.'

'That is excellent. Just what I had hoped to hear. How much did he offer?'

'A cottage in the country,' said Alice, wrinkling her nose.

'We can do better than that. I will have a talk with Mr Sellop.'

'No. Wait. A man has been sent from St Kitts, a black steward who once served my mother. He has brought letters and a book—Oh, do sit down, Mr Christopher. I have so much to explain. Now listen, this Josephus was actually present at my mother's wedding.'

'You have a *witness*? Then everything is plain sailing.'

'I do hope so indeed, but it is not quite so simple.' And Alice poured out everything that had happened, and told him of the man, the poetry book and the locket. She was a little incoherent (for her), and Mr Christopher had to take her over her story several times. He showed a marked interest in the details. 'It is a great pity that you did not bring Josephus here with you today.'

'He is not well. But what do you think? Is his word acceptable in an English court? If only he spoke English better! We should almost need an interpreter.'

'I feel I must see him,' said Mr Christopher, 'to judge for myself. And I must get him to sign a sworn statement, and I very much wish to look at the things he has brought. Tell me about them again, Miss Alice.' She did so.

Then Mr John Gorman appeared at the door of the

169

room, leading the priest and showing signs of agitation. 'You do understand, Father?' he was saying. 'Just the sight of you, in her present state, would frighten Violet to death ...'

'May I go upstairs?' came the voice of Marianne. 'I am sorry we have been so long, but Phoebe insisted on changing her dress.' And there was the maid in the hall with a huge starched white apron crackling at every move, a bundle of linen strips under one arm, and a stone bottle of cordial under the other.

'A black!' came a voice from above in deep-toned amazement.

'Where the young mistress?' demanded Phoebe in a business-like way.

'No black hands are going to touch a child of mine!' said John Gorman rather wildly.

'Why not?' Marianne drew herself up to her fullest height. 'Black hands brought me into the world and so they shall my own babies if ever I become a mother. And black arms, let me tell you, are the greatest comfort in the world when you are small and sick. Control yourself, Mr Gorman! Phoebe is renowned as a *sage-femme* across four parishes. She is clean, she is Christian and she has never tasted gin. What more do you want?'

'Send her upstairs,' called Mrs Gorman, as a wail of anguish floated out of a room behind her. 'Father! We need you.'

'You will oblige me by staying here, Father,' said John Gorman, propelling the priest back into the room. 'Alice. Miss—er—er—forgive me if I seem overwrought. I should have offered you some refreshment.'

'We really must go,' said Alice, who could not face another session with the attorney under the basilisk eye of the priest. 'It is cruel to stay and occupy your mind at such a time.' Her eye caught that of Mr Christopher who, obliging man, went quietly out through the front door. Alice and Marianne soon followed, leaving the Gormans to deal with their troubles in privacy.

170

CHAPTER FIFTEEN

After the alarming events of the day, Alice and Marianne felt entitled to excuse themselves from a concert and a very dull reception. 'Shall I tell Laura that I have a slight fever?' Marianne enquired of Alice as she bent over a small note.

'No, do not do that in case she feels it her duty to come and see you. It is a miracle we have escaped a scene after what Clara overheard this morning.'

'Very well. I have a headache,' Marianne wrote swiftly, 'and you, my dear Alice, feel unable to leave my side.'

'It is Josephus who has the slight fever,' Alice explained. 'I went up to see if your treatment had cured him, and he is much worse than he was this morning. I wonder—do you think he would respond to a little elm-bark embrocation?'

'He may have a touch of malaria, in which case quinine would be better,' said Marianne. 'I have some by me. We will give him a few drops on a spoon.'

By morning, however, the old man was not showing any signs of improvement, and Alice was worried when she joined Marianne in her room. 'I wish Phoebe were back,' she said. 'Josephus looks so lost and sad up there with no-one to talk to him, and his language is getting a little wild. I can hardly understand him at all.'

'Phoebe came home just now. All is well, they have a son, and Phoebe has gone to sleep with a purse with twenty guineas in it.'

'Splendid! That is good news. How pleased they all must be.'

'Phoebe is pleased too. She can buy enough land for an orchard now and get herself a husband. Remind me to write to my factor, Alice.'

171

'When she wakes up, will you ask her to go to Josephus? He needs comforting, and he is in no fit state to go and see Mr Christopher, which Mr Christopher is anxious for him to do—though why I cannot say. Oh yes, he wants to get a signed statement from him.'

'The question is not *why*, but *how*,' said Marianne. 'Josephus does not sound well enough to be moved, yet Geoffrey and Laura have forbidden the attorney to come here. And I cannot see Mr Brown offering to help us again so soon, can you?'

'Suppose I told Laura that I was sending for the apothecary to scc Josephus, and sent for Mr Christopher instead?' asked Alice. 'He would be shown upstairs without meeting Laura—for she would never bother to attend to the apothecary, especially with all the fuss going on in the house about the ball—and we could interview Mr Christopher, perhaps in my room, for as long as we liked.'

'My dear Alice!' cried Marianne with some awe. 'How you have come on! To think—I have only been here a few weeks, but I swear when I arrived you would no more think of going to Africa than of deceiving Laura, and conniving to receive a visitor whom your brother does not allow and conversing with a young man *in your bedroo*m! My dear, staid cousin, how you are improved!'

'Good gracious!' cried Alice. Every word Marianne said was true! 'Well,' she went on with spirit, 'I had no idea then that Geoffrey could be so brutal or that Laura was a bullying monster under her genteel airs. If I had not opposed them, they would have destroyed me utterly —and if I have to act underhand, it is because they will not allow me to fight in the open. All the same,' Alice bit her lip guiltily, 'my dear mother would have been mortified if she had known.'

Marianne only laughed, and the page scratched on the door with a note from Laura. 'This is an improvement,' said Marianne. 'Soon we shall be communicating by the penny post.'

'Laura is not well this morning and will be keeping to her room,' Alice reported.

'*Tant mieux*,' said Marianne.

'But wait—oh no! She talked to Mr Bunne at the concert last night, and she has arranged for him to call. Mr Bunne! Oh Marianne, what am I to do about him? Laura requests me to see him—listen, it is worse than that, "Sir Geoffrey commands that you give Mr Bunne the courtesy of an interview. The footman has been informed that he is to admit Mr Bunne, alone, to see you in the small sitting-room when he arrives!"'

'Well, you can refuse to see him,' said Marianne candidly, 'and then there will be an immense fuss and tears and anger—quite enough to poison the atmosphere for our ball, I should think. Or else you can let him have his say and then firmly refuse him and the thing is finished. Laura may make a scene, but even she and Geoffrey cannot force you to marry against your will.'

'You are right. Very well, I will see him. What is the procedure in these cases?' asked Alice half-laughing. 'Do I now seat myself in state in the small sitting-room and wait for the single gentleman to be ushered in? He may not come for hours! Advise me, Marianne. I have never been approached so formally before.'

But Marianne's eyes had narrowed. 'One single gentleman is as good as another,' she said, 'and Laura is staying in her room. We will send for Mr Christopher instantly, Alice. Where is my writing desk? Where is Phoebe? Oh, of course, I had forgotten—she is asleep. Who can take a letter for me? Can I trust that pink-faced footman with the lovely thick dark hair?'

'John would be better. How quick-witted you are, Marianne!' Alice had to admire yet again the way her cousin seized any chance that proffered itself.

'I have asked him to come as soon as he gets my note,'

173

Marianne said, 'so we must not lose time. You will have to help me dress, Alice, as Phoebe is not here.'

Alice looked round for a chemise. There seemed to be no neat pile of undergarments such as was placed on a chair in her bedroom overnight.

'Where are your clothes, Marianne?' she asked.

'In the press, I think.'

'All clean ones this morning?'

'Of course,' said her cousin, who had climbed out of bed and was washing herself shiveringly at a large china basin. 'That housemaid did not remember to bring me warm water.'

'Do you mean you wear clean underclothes every day?' marvelled Alice.

'Why yes. Do you mean that you do not?'

'No indeed! I normally change my chemise and petticoats once a week—more often if it is necessary, of course. But think of all the piles of washing if we all put quite clean things on every day!'

'The washing is done every day. I cannot see that it makes much difference,' said Marianne.

'Every day! Our washing is done once a week, normally on a Monday.'

'What strange customs you have in England!' cried Marianne, much struck. 'I call that quite filthy. In the tropics I can assure you that it would be most unwholesome to live like that,' and she wrinkled her nose. 'Besides, what do you do with all the dirty clothes waiting for Monday?'

'They stay in big baskets,' Alice told her. 'And at Holt Lacey—where sometimes in the winter we cannot wash the linen for weeks at a time if the weather is bad, there is a special room where all the baskets are stored until we get good drying weather again.'

'There are certain aspects of living in England which I find very much against my taste,' said Marianne. 'But please find me a bodice, Alice. It is cold standing here.'

'There doesn't seem to be a chemise at all.'

'Here,' said the heiress, pulling a scrap of cambric from the cupboard. 'It buttons down the back. Can you fasten it for me?'

'Marianne, you've got it on inside out.'

'No, I haven't. Do hurry up, Alice. Mr Christopher will not take long to get here.'

'But the frills are *inside*.'

'That is where they are meant to be,' said Marianne, looking down the front of her with satisfaction. She was very slight, and that curved bosom which is so necessary above a tiny waist would have been sadly flat if her gowns had followed her figure. The inside of her bodice, however, was stitched with a multitude of little shaped frills which completely made up for the deficiency. With her background more attuned to Paris than to London, Marianne took such augmentation for granted. To Alice, it seemed to verge on cheating.

'You will have to pull very hard,' Marianne told her as she slipped on a diminutive pair of stays. 'I have the waists of my gowns made half an inch too small, and even then I do not like them to fit too closely.' She clung to the bedpost while Alice manfully struggled with the long stay laces. 'Put your foot in the small of my back if it helps,' said Marianne. 'Phoebe often has to.'

Her drawers, Alice was relieved to see, were of orthodox cut, though so heavily trimmed that Alice thought it must cause some discomfort when she walked. Her stockings were white openwork silk, and her boots of blue cloth were so tight that it took both of them working with a long shoe horn to squeeze her feet inside. She had adopted the English crinoline, but Alice noticed that Phoebe had sewn an extra band of red cloth round the hem, with lace on the inside for good measure.

A blue cotton frock of deceptive simplicity was dropped over all, and then Marianne sat down at the dressing table to arrange her own hair.

'Don't all those starched frills scratch you?' asked

175

Alice. Her own toilet had been much simplified, and on the whole she thought she looked no worse for it.

'Pride must suffer pain,' said Marianne sententiously. 'Have you never heard that, Alice? It is a phrase that never leaves Great-Aunt Euphemie's lips.'

Whilst they awaited the attorney's coming, Alice went up to see Josephus and found him shivering and moaning in his bed. It was difficult to tell what he was saying —but then, it had never been easy for Alice. She asked the housekeeper to come and assist her in dosing the old man with a mild febrifuge, and was trying to get him to take a little weak broth when Marianne sent word that she was needed below.

'Can we get Josephus downstairs to the small sitting-room?' she asked the housekeeper. 'Someone is there who needs to question him.'

They tried, but it was impossible. Every attempt to move him brought on a fit of gabbling excitement and Alice had not the heart to go on. In the end, Mr Christopher was requested to come upstairs, which he did with great good humour. Josephus was quiet when Marianne stood beside him and smoothed his brow. But, alas! he was little use as a witness. Alice bit her lip with chagrin as all hope of getting a sworn statement out of him died away. His answers to the attorney's questions were not clear, he lost track of his words and faltered. The locket was carefully examined, but what use was a betrothal gift when the question was one of marriage? A tear crept down from the corner of Alice's eye.

'Never mind,' said Marianne to cheer her up, 'the words in this book are quite clear—look, Mr Christopher. It seems the rest of the page has been torn away, but you can read quite clearly, "*on the day of our marriage!*" There! Stay, stay, Josephus, *soit tranquille.* No-one is going to rob you of it. We'll put it back into your hand.'

Alice wiped her eyes. 'Really I am most deeply obliged to you, Mr Christopher,' she said. 'Meeting in shrubberies and strange drawing-rooms! And now a trip to the attics! How many attorneys would have taken so much trouble?'

'I have enjoyed it,' he said simply.

'We should go now,' she said. 'Josephus is wasting his strength,' and she sighed deeply as she led the way down to the small sitting-room. 'I am sorry now that we bothered you to come.'

'Nevertheless, the visit has not been wasted,' Mr Christopher said.

'Do you mean that my Mama's inscription in that book will convince a judge in a court?'

'Not precisely,' the attorney said. 'But it opens up a fresh line of thought. I strongly advise you, Miss Alice, to let me send another clerk to Nevis to look for fresh evidence.'

'Is that necessary? Can we not wait until the first one returns?'

'I would like to send one now, immediately.'

'Very well. You agree, do you not, Marianne?'

'Of course. We wish to do everything necessary. But I do not quite understand. All this will take two months at least and in the meantime Sir Geoffrey will offer a settlement. Is Alice not to accept it?'

'By no means.'

Marianne gave him a thoughtful look. 'I do not think this advice is what you would have given my cousin last week,' she said. 'Yet you have seen how old and frail Josephus is. Suppose he never recovers and Alice has no witness?'

'I cannot offer you new hope exactly,' he said. 'And yet I feel the position has been changed. If Sir Geoffrey makes an offer of money to Miss Alice, I think she should ask for time to consider. Or refer him to me, and I will stall on her behalf. A further check must be made.'

'Alice must not lose her chance of a comfortable pro-vision while messages go backwards and forwards to

177

Nevis,' said Marianne. 'After all, is not Great-Aunt Euphemie conducting her own search there?'

'I will do as you instruct me, of course,' said Mr Christopher.

'Then please continue with your efforts in the West Indies if you feel it worthwhile,' cut in Alice. For what use was money if a shameful origin made her an unsuitable wife for anyone well born? But was there any use in thinking about that now ... ?

The footman who showed Mr Christopher to the door announced another caller. Not being of the brightest intellect, he could not remember whether Lady Lacey's orders had concerned one gentleman or one at a time.

'Mr Aloysius Bunne,' he announced with difficulty.

'Miss Alice!' cried Mr Bunne, 'I am delighted to find you at home.'

Marianne rose, made a slight bow, and turned towards the door.

'Don't leave me, Marianne,' begged Alice. 'Stay! Don't go away ... Mr Bunne, I do not feel that there is anything of advantage that we can say to one another—Marianne!'

But her cousin deserted her, her suitor approached, took her hand and begged to be allowed to speak. Alice acceded with the best grace she could muster, wishing only to get it done. She was not inexperienced at turning away unwanted offers, but Mr Bunne was very different from the fortune hunters that had besieged her in former days; his disinterested chivalry merited respect at least.

Mr Bunne began by giving his reasons for wishing to get married, sketched a brief outline of his financial circumstances and the fact that his sister lived permanently under his own roof. His fancy then took wings and he expanded on the theme of love and the attractions which had placed Alice so highly in his esteem. He dwelt on her charitable inclinations, her good sense and her strong wish to help the underprivileged, all in terms

178

which amazed his listener. Alice could only believe that he had come to see what he wished to see, it was so far from reality. Not that Alice was uncharitable herself, but she strongly believed in providing dry houses, strong boots and sunday schools where the village children could learn their alphabets and get a hot bun apiece, rather than far-flung enterprises among the heathen. She tried to stop him when he paused for breath, but Mr Bunne would not be stopped. With a final reference to the leper colony which he had the honour to support, Mr Bunne proudly and happily asked whether the ardent passion burning in his breast could ever hope to kindle a spark in Alice's bosom.

Alice told him that his sentiments, whilst most gratefully received, were entirely unreciprocated and could never be returned.

Mr Bunne was amazed.

Alice asked him kindly to excuse her since there were many things to do in the house with the approaching ball.

'Alice,' said Mr Bunne, breathing heavily. 'I may call you Alice, may I not? My dearest Alice, I have not made myself clear.' He came towards her and prepared to go down on his knees.

'Mr Bunne!' cried Alice, rising and stepping out of his way. 'I have not given you permission to use my name—and *I* have not made *myself* clear. I thank you for your attentions. I am grateful for your kindness. But I am convinced that you are completely mistaken as to my character and that we should never agree.'

'No, no!' he cried gladly. 'You must not let your modesty stand in your way. Trust me, my dear Alice. I will guide your every action, and you shall find that soon our minds, like our hearts, will be as one.'

Alice managed to repress a shudder. 'Mr Bunne,' she said, taking refuge behind the sofa, 'you must believe that I know what I am about. I cannot love you. I do not wish to marry you. You have been most kind, but I beg that you will now go away.'

'Sweet . . .' he tried to get hold of her hand. 'Such maidenly shrinking only adds to your charms. But yield a little. Come and lean on me. You need not fear. Your brother knows of my addressing you and gives us his approval. Doubt no longer, Alice. Say you will be mine.'

'Mr Bunne,' said Alice quite savagely. 'I cannot be yours. Your way of life is not one that I would ever choose for my own. I cannot marry you. I will not marry you. I wish you would find some other girl more of your way of thinking and marry her and leave me alone.'

He stared at her and his mouth fell open. 'Do you mean to refuse me?' he asked without quite believing it.

'Yes, Mr Bunne. I am sorry to cause you pain, but I hope you will soon recover.'

He shook his head sadly. 'I do not understand you,' he said. 'A lady of your sense and discretion could never act this way. I make no demand for fortune. I ask no questions of birth and I offer you freely a half of all that I possess.'

'Mr Bunne,' said Alice wearily, 'would you have me give my hand without my heart?'

'The heart would follow as a matter of course,' he said. 'If that is all that stands in your way, do not let a girlish yearning for romance prevent you from taking a very wise step. My friends think I am a fool. Your brother—how can I express it?—*jumped* at my offer. Your head must tell you that it is the best you are ever likely to receive. Miss Alice—Alice—'

'I beg you to oblige your friends and disoblige my brother by putting all thought of this out of your head. It is impossible. I could never be brought to consent. Can I make myself clearer Mr Bunne?'

He was very deeply offended, and stood red-faced, as if wondering whether to renew the attack. This was not

180

the way the natives of Papua received the gift of warm apparel.

'I shall leave you.' Alice said, 'and go to my room.'

'No, no!' he put up his hand. 'I shall leave you, Miss Alice. And I hope that you will not bitterly regret the decision you have taken today.'

They bowed. He left the room and Alice sank into a chair. From a worldly point of view, of course, Mr Bunne had been right, although it was not perhaps polite for him to have expressed it, but Alice felt she would far rather have a tiny cottage near Holt Lacey.

Clara, who must have been on the watch, came tripping into the room as soon as the front door had closed on Mr Bunne. 'Well?' she asked impertinently, 'when is it to be?'

'I do not know what you mean,' said Alice quite untruthfully.

'When are you going to become Mrs Bunne?' asked Clara with an unfortunate smirk. 'You'll have to get him to buy a new coat for the wedding, Alice. Those long skirts went out with King William!'

Alice bit her lip, but was saved from a sharp rejoinder by the entry of Marianne. 'If you would excuse us, Clara, there are some things which I would like to discuss with my cousin.'

'Laura sent me,' said Clara, bridling, 'and I am sure I have as much right to go where I want in this house as you and Marianne.'

Alice flushed. For two pins, she felt, she would box Clara's ears. She drew in a breath to say something stifling, when the footman opened the door and announced the arrival of Mr Brown. Normally Percy was on such easy terms that he would have come in like a member of the family, but this was the third single gentleman that had arrived that morning, and the footman had worked it out that Her Ladyship's orders must have been in the plural after all.

'Well?' demanded Clara again. 'What am I to tell Laura?'

'Nothing,' said Alice.

'Clara, please leave us for a while,' said Percy brusquely. 'There are some things which I have to say to Alice and to Miss St George.'

'No, I won't go away just because everybody orders me about,' said the unfortunate Clara. 'And you've got no reason to be cross with me, Percy. I know things about you that you wouldn't like other people to know.'

Her outraged brother stared at her down his nose. 'Hold your tongue, Miss,' he said, 'And leave the room.'

'I won't go until Alice tells me,' said Clara crossly.

'Tells you what?'

'Tells me that she's going to marry Mr Bunne. Laura sent me to find out. And as for you, Percy Brown, you can stop talking to me as though I was still a child, so there!'

'*Are* you going to marry Mr Bunne?' asked Percy turning to Alice with a frown. 'If so, this puts quite a different complexion on . . .'

'No, I am not,' said Alice decidedly.

'Oh—you liar!' cried Clara.

'Clara!' thundered her brother. 'How dare you use that word?'

'Well she is! Mr Bunne came here an hour ago especially to ask her,' Clara shrilled.

'And I refused him,' Alice said. 'Please go and tell Laura so, with my compliments, of course.'

'You didn't!' Brother and sister were both astounded. After a moment Clara rushed off to take the disastrous news to Lady Lacey.

'Alice, you must have taken leave of your senses,' said Percy in deeply concerned tones. 'Mr Bunne is a thoroughly respectable man with a good income and a place of his own, apart from his seat in Parliament. How could you turn down such a fortunate way out of all your troubles?'

'They are my troubles, Percy, and I must get out of them the best way I feel fit.'

'He would give you independence, a good home, his name—Alice, you must reconsider.'

'You are not my brother, Percy,' Alice said. 'And there is no reason why I should receive advice from you.'

'I believe you had something important to say to us, Mr Brown,' said Marianne.

His shocked eyes left Alice. 'Yes, I do!' he cried, remembering. 'Miss St George—Alice—I would never have believed it of you. You have grossly deceived me! I feel I have been used as—as—as a parlour tool!'

The new footman flung open the door with pride. Everything was going like clockwork. Single gentlemen arrived almost upon the heels of each other. 'Mr Matthew Vale,' he announced proudly.

CHAPTER SIXTEEN

'Parlour tool!' said Matthew Vale, coming in and surveying the three faces keenly. 'What an interesting expression. Do explain yourself, Brown.'

'It is nothing,' said Percy, turning shame-facedly away.

'He refers,' said Marianne with dancing eyes, 'to a rendezvous which he arranged for us with Alice's attorney.'

'You too?' asked Mr Vale, much amused. 'Well, well. This is a veritable hotbed of intrigue.'

'I don't know what you mean,' said Percy, who had no idea how deeply the newcomer had been involved in Alice's affairs. 'But this is not the place to talk of it.'

'Why not?' asked Marianne mischievously. 'Alice and I are not ungenerous, Mr Brown. We do not wish to hide from the world our esteem for those who have been so gallant as to help us in our problems.'

'Help you!' Percy turned on her. 'Of course I was prepared to help you with small difficulties, but I did not know that you were preparing to drag my sister's name through the courts! You should have told me. How could two young ladies think of such a thing?'

'Laura will not be mentioned,' Alice said quietly, but Matthew Vale had already begun.

'Surely you do not expect Miss Alice to sit quietly by whilst your sister and her brother strip her of all the worldly possessions her father wished her to have?'

'I don't know what business it is of yours!' cried Percy, turning on him.

The door flung open and Clara burst in. 'You are to go to Laura at once, Alice,' she said. 'Oh, excuse me, Mr Vale, I did not see you had come.'

'You are not being fair to Alice,' Marianne told Percy exactly as if there had been no interruption. 'If she had been a man, you would condemn her for sitting down under gross injustice and doing nothing to save herself at all.'

'It is *not* an injustice,' said Percy, in tones that he never expected to use towards Miss St George.

'Laura will be angry if you do not come at once, Alice,' said Clara, 'and she is angry enough as it is.'

'Please tell Laura that we have guests,' said Alice, 'but I will come as soon as I am free.'

'I think the ladies have a point,' Matthew said to Percy, thereby offending him even more.

'You'd do much better to come now,' said Clara.

'Oh, go to your room,' Percy told his importunate sister, 'and leave us alone.'

'You've no right to speak to me like that!' Clara flung back at him. 'I'll tell Laura what you did yesterday, just see if I don't!' and she flounced out.

'I seem to have come at an unfortunate time,' said Mr Vale, much enjoying himself.

'I am sorry, Sir, that you should have got involved in our affairs,' Percy turned on him crossly, 'and would suggest that perhaps another morning might be more suitable for your call.'

'But I particularly wished to see the ladies, if I might be allowed, to engage their promise of dances for the ball tomorrow.'

'Then I wish you good day,' said Percy in a huff. But he was too young and he had been too annoyed to omit a parting shot. 'I shall not ask you to dance with me, Miss St George,' he said loftily. 'Nor you, of course, Alice. If I had known that you were going to turn me into a traitor to my sister, I would never have stained my hands with your affairs!'

'Hoity-toity!' murmured Mr Vale as the door slammed behind the departing Percy.

'What a morning!' sighed Alice. 'I fear that you have lost an admirer, Marianne.'

'What a shame,' her cousin sighed in unison. 'I had

such a desire to be the wife of a Lord of the Treasury. What is a Lord of the Treasury, and why is it so much below an under secretary? No, don't explain it to me, Mr Vale. I am sure it is tedious beyond words. But I am not the greatest loser, Alice,' she teased with a quite unpardonable lack of discretion. 'You also have turned a lover away. Poor Mr Bunne!'

'*Please*, Marianne,' begged Alice, turning deepest red.

The door opened yet again to admit a freshly risen Phoebe. 'Miss Marianne,' she said, 'better you come quickly. That Josephus he toss and turn so I never control him. And he talk plenty now—maybe all the things you go want to hear.'

'I will come at once,' said Alice, gladly getting up from her chair.

'Better Miss Marianne, case you no understand what that man saying,' Phoebe told her, and Marianne also sprang up. 'Yes, of course. Do not come, Alice. Josephus is used to me and if you were there it might confuse him,' and with a brief farewell to Matthew Vale she ran from the room.

In acute embarrassment Alice turned to the window and sought for some general remark that would restore the tone of polite conversation. Surely Mr Vale would go now that Marianne was no longer here and they two were left completely unchaperoned? But Matthew Vale gave no time for generalities.

'Is it true?' he demanded, striding across to her.

'Is what true?'

'That Bunne offered marriage to you?' He seemed extremely angry. 'That prosing dotard! I wonder that he had the impertinence.'

'Mr Bunne has been extremely kind and generous,' said Alice, honour-bound.

'Kind! A dull elderly bore—to shackle your youth and beauty to his charity meetings and his tracts. Kind! He should be cast in irons,' said Mr Vale with quite unjustified wrath.

The room started to blur in front of Alice's eyes. Surely this anger could only mean that Mr Vale cared very much what happened to her?

'So what did you tell him?' he demanded, roughly grasping her arm.

'Mr Vale!' cried Alice weakly. 'You have no right!'

He laughed. 'No right!' he said. 'How true!' And flinging away from her he paced up and down the floor. 'Dearest Alice,' he began, in the grip of strong emotion.

'What?' she asked in a very small voice.

'Dearest Alice,' he repeated, and swung her round to face him. 'You must know that you are dearer to me than anyone else in the world.'

'I did not know,' she whispered. 'I thought you were getting to care for Marianne.'

He laughed again, but this time in genuine amusement. 'That schemer?' he asked. 'I would not get tied up in her web if she were the only woman in London. No wonder young Brown has found her out—it was only a question of time. But you, Alice, have had me at your feet these four months past. Did you not know?'

'It isn't possible,' said Alice, and her bosom rose and fell.

'No, there's the devil of it,' he said, breaking away again and giving no apology for swearing. 'I have no right to speak, as you so justly said. Bunne, damn him, can ask you to be his wife and offer you a home and comfortable living, while I—oh, Alice, what are we to do?'

Her heart expanded and her eyes shone. Never had she looked more lovely. But then her strong sense of what was right took hold. 'Mr Vale,' said Alice. 'I will forget what you have just said . . .'

'No. By all the saints, I love you.'

'But it is hopeless. You can see. You must go off and find some young lady of whom the Duke of Severn would approve, and I . . .'

'Never.'

'. . . must even marry Mr Bunne, if I am driven to it,' she finished.

'You do not know what you are saying.'

'I do. I do. How could you think of marrying me when it would drive your uncle to disown you?'

He hit his fist against the mantleshelf and sank his head upon it. 'What sort of a man am I?' he asked himself through clenched teeth, 'when I have less to offer the woman I love than my own coachman?'

'Don't blame yourself,' begged Alice. 'My birth is the cause of all the trouble.'

'We could go away together,' he said. 'Get married and live in some cheap place abroad, where I could turn my hand to some sort of work—would you do that, Alice?' and crossing to her once more, he seized her hands.

She shook her head.

'Is it not good enough for you? Do you not love me enough to take the risk?'

'I love you too much,' said Alice with no trace of maiden shame. 'How could I do it to you? Drag you down from a high position and great expectations to some small hovel in a foreign town? Make you give up Parliament and friends and leisure for empty poverty? What would people think of me? What would I think of *myself*?'

'I think you are the most desirable girl in the world,' he said simply.

Alice drew one deep breath. She could not stop her pulse from racing, but she could control her words. 'This must be the last time we talk upon the subject, Mr Vale. You must go. Believe me, I am profoundly grateful for the—the sentiments which you have uttered, but I will not consent to anything that would finish all your prospects in the world.'

'Sanctimonious claptrap!' he growled fiercely.

She gave a little startled gasp of surprise and mirth. He was holding her hands as if they were straws and he

189

was a drowning man. The very strongest sense of propriety could not make her want to withdraw them.

'One thing,' he said. 'Understand me. No Bunne or any other prating fool is going to snatch you away from me before this affair has been finally settled.' And seizing her in his arms he kissed her firmly on the mouth and then quitted the room.

Alice dropped into a chair and started to shake all over. Her cousin was with her again before she had had time to get her feelings under control.

'Alice, we really must send for that apothecary now,' she began. 'Josephus is delirious and in high fever— well! What has happened to put you in such a state? Has Laura been at you?' she demanded fiercely. 'This is the outside of enough! I shall go to her and ...'

'No, no,' cried Alice. 'It is not Laura!' And after a few moments hesitation, she decided that her cousin could not be left in the dark. 'It is Mr Vale,' she confessed. 'He has—has said that he cares for me.'

'And about time too!' cried Marianne gladly, dispersing every little fear that had been causing Alice such gloom. 'If he had not done so, I should have had a very low opinion of him. So you are to be married! That is the best end to it all.'

'No, no,' Alice replied. 'Of course I refused him. How could I bring such a cloud on his prospects? Of course his uncle would never allow him to marry me.'

'So he will marry you without his uncle's permission,' said Marianne stoutly, 'and when your own affairs are settled, there will be enough to live on till the old man dies.'

'I cannot do it to him, Marianne. He would have to find employment. We would have to go and live at B-Boulogne.'

'*Quelle blague!*' said Marianne crudely. 'Enough of the Lacey inheritance will come to you one way or another to pay the baker, Alice, and once you are married the old duke may well come round.'

190

'It must not be,' said Alice steadfastly, wiping away the tears which had begun to fall. 'No one shall say that I separated a man from his friends and his family and his career.'

'My dear Alice, you are talking like a French novel and I refuse to listen any further,' said her cousin. 'And do help me with Josephus. He is a Beauregarde servant, after all, and I am responsible for him.'

'Of course. Forgive me,' said Alice contritely. As they hurried out of the room they met Sir Geoffrey who had just come through the front door. 'There is no sign of luncheon,' he said, 'and I could hardly get in for boxes of champagne. Where is Laura? I am meeting the Minister at half-past-two and a pile of papers has been removed from my room. What is the matter with every-thing?'

'It is the ball,' Marianne explained, while Alice hung back to hide her tear-stained face. 'I believe luncheon has been put back. Would you like me to enquire, Sir Geoffrey?'

'I will do it. There is no reason for you or Alice to be troubled. This is Laura's work,' he replied unexpectedly. His manner was strange—a mixture of the nervous and the deferential.

The girls went upstairs and set in motion the sum-moning of the apothecary. 'I wonder what has made your brother so polite all of a sudden?' whispered Marianne. 'Is it because we have a witness to your mother's wedding?'

'Just wait until he has spoken to Laura,' Alice whis-pered back. 'He will get into one of his rages with me then.'

But that was not the case. When they met in the dining-room and stood with plates of cold chicken in their hands for all the chairs were heaped high with tablecloths and napkins, they found that Sir Geoffrey had forced his wife to dress and come down for the meal, and she confined her feelings to angry glares in

191

Alice's direction. Clara's impertinences also were cut short by her brother-in-law with the result that Clara relapsed into a fine fit of sulks and the burden of conversation fell upon Marianne. She gave them details of Josephus' fever with prattling facility and said how sad she felt with the old man being so very ill so very far from home.

'You will visit him, of course,' said Sir Geoffrey sternly to his wife.

'He is no concern of mine!' flashed back Lady Lacey.

'Nevertheless, he is an inmate in this house and the servant of our own guest,' said Sir Geoffrey, bowing towards Marianne. His wife shot him a puzzled look, but her surprise was quite equalled by Alice's and her cousin's. To what did they owe this excessive courtesy? There was a great deal of unease under Sir Geoffrey's gracious manner. And how he had aged over the last few weeks! He had been an upright, fresh-faced gentleman who held his head thrown back. Today he was bowed, his colour had gone and he looked a man of fifty.

'I should like the pleasure of a few minutes conversation with you, Alice,' he said when the meal was ended. 'Shall we go to the drawing-room?'

'Not there, Geoffrey. The carpets are rolled up and the maids are polishing the floor.'

'Then in my room ...' he ushered her in.

Alice steeled herself. If he was going to try the effect of gentle persuasion, she was not going to let it undermine her resolve. 'Let me warn you, Geoffrey,' she said as soon as they were alone, 'that nothing you can say will persuade me to accept Mr Bunne.'

'Mr Bunne? No indeed!' he replied. 'I hope we can do better than that for you, eh, Alice?'

'Laura thinks I should grasp at his offer,' Alice blurted out in her surprise.

'Laura knows nothing whatever about it,' said the baronet loftily, 'although she has your very best interest at heart, of course, Alice. As have I, it is needless to say.'

Alice gave a noncommittal murmur.

'Your future is much on my mind, dear sister, and I should like to apologize if I spoke a little harshly the other day. There have been many things on my mind.' And he pulled at his whiskers and contemplated his foot.

Again Alice murmured deprecatingly. But her mind leapt to an instant conclusion. Geoffrey was about to make her an offer of settlement and what was she to do? Mr Christopher had strongly advised her not to be talked into accepting.

'Considering my father's wishes,' went on Sir Geoffrey, dropping into his parliamentary style and rounding his phrases as his head went back, 'and not forgetting the gratitude I must feel towards the lady who acted as my mama for so many years—although of course,' he remembered, 'we should continue to omit her name from family records; but bearing in mind, as I say, the obligations which duty and affection lay upon me, the past and present bonds of loving interest between our two selves, which go back to the cradle in your case and to early youth in mine . . .'

'Please come to the point, Geoffrey,' Alice could not help interrupting.

He did not even take offence. 'Yes,' he said. 'Well, Alice, I have come to the conclusion that it would be degrading and unnecessary to allow the differences of opinion between us to be haggled over in a court of law. The name of Lacey should not be so besmirched. Especially in view of what our father expressly intended.'

'Our father wished me to have all the Lacey inheritance,' said Alice, not mincing matters.

'Quite. That of course is impossible. You can see—anybody can see—that it is just and right that I should hold the Lacey home in the same way that I carry the Lacey name.'

Alice sighed. Her brother was not prepared, it seemed, to part with much for the sake of the family's fair name. She wondered drearily how much he proposed to buy her off with. One thousand pounds? Two thousand? Three?

'Nevertheless, the wishes of a parent are sacrosanct. Or almost.' Sir Geoffrey corrected himself. 'I wish to retain the house and park at Holt Lacey, but as for the rest, my dear Alice, I am prepared to hand it over to you.'

There was a moment of stunned silence. 'I don't understand you, Geoffrey,' Alice said at last.

'Really? I had thought I made myself quite clear.'

'Do you mean that if I tell Mr Christopher to stop opposing your claim to have father's will changed . . .'

'And call off all legal proceedings whatsoever,' added her prudent brother.

'That you will give me the Bath and Bristol holdings?'

The baronet nodded. It hurt him, but he nodded.

'And the railway shares and the London property?'

'Yes.'

'Including *this house*?' asked Alice, unable to credit it.

'Yes,' said her brother, drawing the admission out between his teeth.

'What about the Home Farm and the other farms near Holt Lacey?' asked his sister. It wasn't that she was greedy—she was so astonished that she really wanted to know the extent of her brother's extraordinary proposals.

'I think I should need to keep the Home Farm in my possession for family use,' said Sir Geoffrey. 'The Wiltshire farms would go to you.'

Alice was quite dumbfounded. 'What can I say?' she asked.

'Only say that you agree, my dear sister, and we will get a lawyer to draw up the papers immediately,' said

194

Sir Geoffrey. 'There need be no delay. Matters have dragged on disgracefully as it is.'

'No . . . wait. Forgive me, Geoffrey, but I cannot take it all in in such a hurry. I have to think. What you propose is so different from what I had expected.'

'You must make your mind up quickly for the offer will not stand for ever,' said Sir Geoffrey with a contortion of the mouth.

'But I must consult my attorney.'

'We will keep the attorneys out of this if you please.'

'No, Geoffrey, that is unfair. You always have Mr Sellop to advise you.'

'Not now. He no longer handles the Lacey affairs.'

'Mr Sellop dismissed!' cried Alice in the utmost astonishment. 'But he has been with us for years. Why did you treat an honest old man so, Geoffrey?'

'He made a suggestion which I found outrageous,' said the baronet very stiffly. 'He has nothing to do with us at all. His opinion carries no weight, and he is not authorized to make any pronouncement on our family affairs.' He looked down into her puzzled face. 'Come, Alice,' he said. 'We have always trusted each other, have we not? We do not need the law to intervene between us. This is a generous offer I am making you. Most generous.'

'It is indeed,' breathed Alice.

'Then you should close with it at once. Now. Who knows what tomorrow may bring forth? You cannot always expect to find me in such an open-handed mood,' said he with a ghastly attempt at a smile.

'You must allow me a few days, Geoffrey.'

'No.'

'Two days . . . a night, then? I must at least discuss it with my cousin.'

'You may do that. Miss St George is a young lady who will understand the value of what I propose.'

They parted on the agreement that Alice would let him know her decision within the next twenty-four hours. 'But you are not to bring Mr Christopher in on this,' Sir Geoffrey warned her, 'or my offer is void. The subject is to remain within the family. I have been over-generous as it is.'

Upon which Alice could not but agree with him.

CHAPTER SEVENTEEN

'I cannot go riding,' said Alice, as she met Marianne on the landing. The heiress was wearing a dark green habit and carrying a small whip.

'Oh yes you can,' replied her cousin. 'It is just what you need to give you some colour in your cheeks. You look wretched, Alice. You need fresh air.'

'But I must talk to you. Something so strange has happened.'

'Well we cannot go to my bedroom,' said Marianne, standing aside to give passage to the two sweating footmen who were struggling with a mahogany chaise longue, 'because there are twelve potted palms stored there, and your room is probably filled with crates of chickens. Get changed quickly, Alice. It is a lovely afternoon, and you cannot expect me to share it with Clara. Besides, I half-agreed to meet Lord Locke.'

Alice had to laugh. There were no chickens in her room but there were seven gilt chairs and a yawning Phoebe, who seized upon the chance of dressing Miss Alice to have a good grumble about the disarray in English homes.

They could not speak while the groom was escorting them through the London traffic, but once in the park, Alice was able to explain to Marianne all that had taken place between herself and her brother. 'And what am I to do?' she finished at the end.

'Take it. Accept it immediately. I will go with you and make him repeat his words. Then we will get the lawyers to draw up everything properly. No doubt he has some little scheme in his mind to get your acceptance and then default on his side of the bargain. What a very low opinion of female understanding Geoffrey does have! We will get it all tied up before he can say, Boo!'

'But my name . . . my mother's reputation . . .'

'Your name will not be your own much longer. Mr Vale will see to that.'

'Marianne, you don't understand. I *refused* Mr Vale.'

'Tell it to the Marines!' cried Marianne gaily, and as they were joined by friends, it was impossible to discuss the matter further.

Alice craved time to think and consider. Marianne's advice was excellent, no doubt. Her horse walked along at its own pace while the rider sat deep in thought. Her fortune returned almost entire—her birth still a matter of shame.

The marriage was now perfectly possible, if Mr Vale still wanted to pursue it. They could live in London or Wiltshire—or both—exactly as Matthew preferred. However the duke took offence, Mr Vale would almost inevitably come into the title. He could continue his career in the House of Comons until he was called as Duke of Severn to the House of Lords. And what would she, Alice, be called? *The bastard duchess*? She blushed at the term. It was cruel. But that would not stop men from whispering it at their clubs.

'A very fine afternoon, Miss Alice,' said Lord Locke at her side. She had not seen him approach. Marianne had trotted away to join gayer company and the young man did not seem to have taken it unkindly. His mama was infinitely better informed than Mr Bunne. She had heard that Alice was contesting her right to the Lacey inheritance, and that odds were said to be in the girl's favour. A slight question mark about her birth could not be allowed to outweigh the heavy advantages of all that property, thought Lady Locke. On the contrary, it would be a rod to keep a daughter-in-law in her proper place.

'You know I always did feel a preference for you, Miss

Alice,' said Lord Locke apropos of nothing at all. 'You don't make a fellow feel such a duffer.'

They had to go out that evening, although Alice would have been so glad to stay at home with her thoughts and Marianne generously offered to stay with her. 'But it is a small dinner-party,' Alice explained, 'and I cannot upset dear Lady Arthur's table arrangements. We are asked early, for there may be a division in the House later. Once the gentlemen have gone, perhaps we can come away.'

Phoebe dressed them, but did not accompany Marianne as she was to sit by Josephus' bed.

'I feel very guilty about Josephus,' Alice said. 'My mind has been on other things when I should have been doing more to help.'

'He plenty sick, Miss Alice,' Phoebe agreed. 'Old man like that get fever, got no strength to pull through.'

As they were a little early, the girls decided to wait in the cool front hall rather than converse around the potted palms. The black and white marble tiles were gleaming with polish and Laura had hired six lofty statues of well-draped Grecian nymphs to gaze down from marble pedestals upon the throng that was expected. At the bottom of the staircase, however, a huge, gas chandelier lay in their way. It had been lowered to the floor, and the dark-haired footman was attacking the lustres with a chamois cloth.

'What *are* you doing?' asked Alice.

'Polishing the glass bits, Miss, and fetching up the brasses.'

'At this hour of the day? And where are the maids?'

'Half of them is helping cook, Miss, she's in a terrible temper. And the other half is stripping the master's room for cloaks.'

They took refuge in the porch, waiting for the Laceys.

'Laura has the strangest ideas of household management,' said Alice. 'She seems quite incapable of making up her mind. I haven't been consulted, of course, but I gather she could not decide between a cold buffet or a hot supper. She ordered turkey poults from Norfolk at the very worst time of the year and then decided on salmon when it was too late to countermand the turkeys.'

'So are we to have our supper hot or cold?'

'Both, it seems. With all the disadvantages of some sitting and some standing, and gravies and hot peas fighting against salad with mayonnaise. No wonder cook is annoyed! There is no excuse for such irrational behaviour. The salon should have been opened up and aired last week instead of Monday, and then when the glasses were unpacked and polished and the extra silver cleaned, they could have been stored there out of the way. The linen I always put in the housekeeper's room, but it was properly checked, counted and divided into the right bundles a week before the event, and then one could devote one's mind to the food. Cook could have parboiled the turkeys yesterday and stored them in crocks under wet clothes in the coldest part of the cellars, and then two maids would have been free tomorrow morning to help with arranging the carnations on the flower stands.'

'Spare me!' cried Marianne, throwing up her hands. 'No doubt you find it enthralling, Alice, but to me it would be one big headache.'

'Do you not organize your parties like that at Beauregarde?'

'No. I leave everything to the steward. He has been at it since before I was born. Of course, we do not always seek after something new like you all do in London. The pepper-pot *ragout* at Beauregarde is famous right down the islands. Our guests expect it—it is what they come for, and they like to have it always the same. I must say I find that more restful. And as for flowers—three small piccuns are detailed to rush out and bring in branches of bougainvillea when the first carriage is heard at the bottom of the hill, and there is barely time to push them into vases before they start to wilt.'

Lady Arthur also seemed to have heard about the Lacey law case, for Alice was given a place far higher up the table than a lady of doubtful origin would normally expect. She would not, in fact, have noticed if she had been given a grass mat to sit on, for Matthew Vale was also there, and it took every ounce of control that Alice possessed not to let her eyes stray across the table to his.

'A quiet girl,' said the newly-elected Member for Hampshire, who had heard a great deal about Miss Alice and was disappointed. 'A beauty of course, but very little conversation.'

'They say the Bristol property alone brings in twelve thousand a year,' said Mr Charles Longford wistfully.

When the gentlemen joined the ladies in the drawing-room upstairs, Lady Arthur asked Alice to give them the benefit of some music. It was the most natural thing in the world that Mr Vale, who was near at hand, should offer to turn over the pages when Miss Alice took her seat at the piano. She was so used to taking her turn on such occasions, when young ladies could show how much care papa had put into their education, that she was able to complete her selection from Chopin without disgrace. Each time Mr Vale's form bent over her and his arm brushed hers her heart almost stopped beating, but nobody noticed the *staccato* passages in places where the composer had recommended *legato*.

The Misses Brentford, who found parliamentary dinner-parties a bore, wished to enliven the proceedings with a glee. One of them played, one of them sang and they managed to get the help of a few others, although Alice declined and drew back. A good deal of giggling and chaff and handing round of parts absorbed the group round the piano, and Alice found herself cut off in a large bay window with Mr Vale, behind the instrument and out of view of the rest of the room.

201

Matthew Vale, never a man to waste an opportunity, promptly tilted up her chin and kissed her.

'Oh Mr Vale!' whispered Alice, quite taken aback. 'You should not have done that!'

'Why not? Are we not betrothed?'

'No. That is—we—I mean—Mr Vale, I thought I had refused your gratifying offer.'

'I believe you did,' he said and kissed her again.

'Mr Vale! Someone will see.'

'I hope they do,' he replied. 'I have been behaving like a craven. I want to come out before the world, dear Alice, and proclaim that at last you have a protector. The only thing that prevents me,' he said candidly, 'is that we should both starve.'

'Mr Vale,' said Alice, her colour rising. 'Money need not be a deterrent.' Was that rather a *fast* way of putting it? Taking the lead? Never mind. In a series of rapid, whispered sentences entirely covered by the noisy glee, she told him all that had passed between her and her brother.

'I shall not be quite so well placed as I was before,' she finished conscientiously, 'but there would be a very comfortable provision. We—that is— if it were required, a house in Wiltshire could be enlarged, and there is the Portman Square home, which is quite convenient for Westminster.'

Now that was truly indelicate. Her feelings had betrayed her almost into making a proposal. *Almost?* What could have been more blatant? Alice's cheeks burned, and she hastened to offer some way of retreat to Mr Vale in case he should think that she was leading him on. 'Of course, one of the conditions of acceptance would be that I gave up all further enquiries about my mother. Geoffrey was quite clear about that. If I continue to search for her marriage records, this offer will cease, and with a choice between my name or my fortune, I do not know what to do.'

She stood and studied the carpet and the hot blood

drained slowly from her face. Mr Vale said never a word.

'Hey, nonny, nonny,' carolled Lettice Brentford energetically.

'Are you not pleased at the news?' asked Alice at last.

'No doubt I shall be,' said Mr Vale. 'But at the moment it sticks in my craw that my wife should give up her name to provide me with a roof and bread and butter.'

'Oh Mr Vale!' It was all right! 'That does not matter to me at all, if you do not mind it.'

'I do,' he replied obstinately. 'Not your name, for that is not your fault, but the money. It seems like a bribe.'

She lifted her head. Relief lit up her eyes like candles. 'Would you have let my money stop you when I was Alice Lacey?'

'Not for an instant,' he replied. 'But that was taking no advantage. If I do agree—and I must think more about this, Alice. The first decision is yours. If you decide to put your hand to this shameful treaty, then I could only allow you to do so . . .'

'Yes?'

'Because I cannot help it,' he said ruefully. 'If that is the only way to make you mine, then I can do nothing to prevent you, come what may,' and he enfolded her in his arms.

The last verse of the glee lasted perhaps three minutes, but to Alice it was endless. 'Is it not strange,' she marvelled, 'that Marianne and I have been scampering all over London to find privacy for discussion, and yet you and I find it here in a crowded drawing-room without any effort at all?'

Even when the group finished, they were succeeded by a broad damsel who took her seat at the piano without a glance behind her, and they had a few more minutes together.

'Think about it,' Matthew instructed Alice. 'Sleep on it, and let me know what you decide to do. Your mother's honour is involved and I cannot tell how much that means to you. When you have decided, let me know at once.'

'How different you are from Mr Bunne,' Alice replied. 'He said he would guide my every action until my mind was at one with his.'

Mr Vale said something not quite proper under his breath, then, 'If you decide to close with Sir Geoffrey's offer, I will see him myself. You do not need to cross swords with him ever again. And then I must go straight to the duke—I owe him that. It will mean travelling to Italy. Are you prepared to be left alone, my love? It might take two weeks, but no longer.'

'Oh yes.'

'You must not remain with the Laceys once you have settled with Geoffrey. I do not trust him. There is something about this offer that rings untrue. I cannot place you in the Severn house without setting people's tongues clacking—and that I will not do. Could you go to Mrs Gorman?'

'Yes. Yes, I think so. But there is Marianne.'

'Your cousin can have the pleasure of thinking up some delightful scheme of her own.'

'Mr Vale.'

'*Matthew*. What is it, my love?'

'I think the gentlemen have been summoned back to the House.'

'Perhaps they have.'

'Should you not go with them? Is there not to be a division?'

'Now look here, Alice,' said Matthew Vale firmly. 'You are to have control over your own affairs. God protect me from turning you into a Mrs Bunne! But I have complete say over mine. Is that understood?'

'Yes Matthew,' said Alice meekly.

Laura stayed downstairs when they reached home, for

various servants were still scurrying about, and Her Ladyship had thought of several alterations.

'Oh, I am so tired!' yawned Marianne. 'There is nothing so fatiguing as hearing young ladies sing. But you look happy enough, Alice. *L'amour* suits you, it is plain.'

Alice smiled. 'I must go up and see how Josephus is,' she said, 'before I sleep. Did the apothecary leave medicine for him to take last thing?'

'Phoebe has it,' said Marianne with another huge yawn. 'Send her down to me, will you, Alice?'

Since no gas was laid above the first floor, Alice lit a small bedside candle and went upstairs. Beyond the main bedrooms the carpet ended and plain haircord covered the twisted flight that rose to the attics. She had just reached the bottom of this staircase when she heard footsteps coming down. She paused, and a tall man's figure bumped into her, knocking the candle out of her hand.

'Geoffrey!' exclaimed Alice, blinking in the sudden darkness. The footsteps hurried away. 'John! Is that you?' asked Alice sharply. There was no reply. She groped for the candlestick and then felt her way downstairs again to Marianne's room.

'Where is Phoebe?' asked the heiress, sleepily taking pins out of her hair.

'I didn't reach Josephus' room. A—a—a—man bumped into me. I was . . . alarmed,' said Alice.

'What man? A footman?'

'It could have been. I thought at first it was Geoffrey.'

'Why should your brother go up to the servants' rooms?'

'I must have been mistaken.' Alice relit her candle. 'Please come with me, Marianne,' she begged. 'It sounds stupid, but I feel quite nervous on my own.'

'If I must,' said Marianne. 'But wait while I slip off my crinoline, or I shall stick on those stairs,' and she threw up her skirts to feel for the strings.

They went up together. The upper floors were quite dark.

'Phoebe!' called Marianne. There was no answer. When they reached the top of the winding stairs they could see no light from the open door of the room where Josephus was lying. 'Why have you not got a candle? Phoebe!' They went into the room. The first thing they saw was the black maid, fast asleep in a chair under the window, lost to the world. Then they brought the candle to the bed.

Josephus was lying peacefully on his back. He had pushed off the top part of the blankets, revealing a respectable high-necked nightshirt. He made no movement of recognition when the candle lit up his gentle old face, nor did his eyes blink. They stayed wide open —staring at them.

'Good God! He is dead!' Marianne said. 'Poor Josephus. To have travelled hundreds of miles for this!'

'Marianne,' whispered Alice. 'Why is that pillow lying on the floor beside his head?'

'Why should it not be? Do you mean? Oh, Alice! Who was that man?' she gripped her cousin's arms.

'I don't know. I can't think. Oh, poor, poor Josephus. What are you doing, Marianne?'

The heiress was bending over the bed. Now she straightened up to face Alice. 'The locket is gone!' she said.

CHAPTER EIGHTEEN

By common consent—in which Marianne fully con-
curred—the death of old Josephus was allowed to pass
almost unnoticed on the day of the Lacey's ball. It
would not be right to cancel an important social event
on account of an old man who was not even a member
of the household. Laura did not want to hear anything
about it. Her mind was in a whirl and her body darted
about trying to be in three places at once and doing
nothing properly.

As the weather was hot and as there was no family
to gather from distant counties nor mourning to set the
tailors scurrying for their needles, the body was quietly
taken from the house and interred that very afternoon.

Marianne, Alice and Phoebe followed the coffin to its
quiet grave. Although ladies did not normally attend
funerals, they could not abandon Josephus, so far away
from home, on his last journey.

'Never you cry, Miss Alice,' said Phoebe, patting her
hand as they sat in the carriage. 'Josephus very good
old man, go straight for heaven.'

'Alice, please, please stop crying,' Marianne begged
some hours later. 'It is time to dress for the party and
you look like Mount Misery at the height of the rainy
season.'

'I am sorry,' Alice sniffed.

'Phoebe was right, you know. Josephus had reached
the end of his years, and if he had still been at Beauregarde, he would probably have died just the same.'

'It is not that,' said Alice, sniffing.

'We agreed not to talk about the other thing,' said
Marianne sharply, 'until we can obtain advice.'

'Geoffrey . . .'

'We have no proof. You did not even know that it was

he. You promised to leave it all to Mr Vale, Alice, and stop worrying about it. At least he can find out what time Sir Geoffrey left the House of Commons. What can we do? Two females? Nothing!'

'But the locket ...'

'Listen,' said Marianne urgently. 'We worked it all out, did we not, last night? If Geoffrey murdered Josephus ...'

'Don't say it, Marianne.'

'*Sacre bleu*, it is you who have brought it up again! If Geoffrey killed him, it was to destroy a witness, was it not? That is why the locket was taken too. The thief would not know that the date inside was wrong.'

'Y-yes.'

'So if Geoffrey did it—and we do not *know* he did, do we?'

'No. Oh no.'

'Then he would feel safe now. He would not fear you any more. He could go back to grinding you into the dust.'

'You are quite right, Marianne. It seemed much clearer last night.'

'So he would have withdrawn his offer to you.'

'Yes he would.'

'But he has not done so.'

'No. He asked me just now if I had made up my mind, and I told him I wanted a few hours more time.'

'Much as I despise your brother, I am glad that he is not a murderer,' said Marianne. 'Now do make an effort, Alice. You need not cry for Josephus. You need not shudder for Geoffrey. We have a ball that should provide some pleasant moments, however Laura may have messed up the rest. Mr Vale will be there. Are you not happy at the thought of meeting him?'

Alice stood up and pushed the hair back from her ears. 'It will be such a relief to hear what he thinks about it,' she said. 'My note told him every detail. And in the other matter, he said he would see Geoffrey for me . . .' she gulped.

'What is it now?' asked Marianne quite waspishly.

Alice walked to the wall and lifted down the crucifix that had hung there ever since it was removed from the small sitting-room. 'I will put my mother's things away now,' she said sadly, taking down the portrait of Amelie and the one of Mrs Fitzherbert. 'You will not mind if I remove this icon, Marianne? I should like to shut them all up in a box.'

'You Laceys have a strange passion for starting house-work just as you should be preparing for enjoyment.'

'No. Please do not joke. I know it would be silly to say my mother's picture could see what we were doing . . .'

'Heaven forfend!'

'But I shall not feel comfortable with her around after Mr Vale has spoken to Geoffrey.'

'Do you think she would not want her child to be well married and happy?'

'It is not that. By giving up the fight for her lost name, I feel I have—how do the Americans say it?— *sold her down the river.*'

'Ten thousand abominations!' cried Marianne. 'Will nothing make you content? And why are we wasting time when we should be dressing? Here's Phoebe with the hot water. Phoebe, go to the kitchens—they will be in a turmoil. Get a large cucumber and a cupful of crushed ice. Then take Miss Alice to her room, lay her on the bed, make a cold compress for her eyes and force her to stay still for twenty minutes. And Alice, if you dare shed one more tear, I will never speak to you again.'

They stood at the head of the great curving staircase, Laura in green satin, with emeralds, Marianne in pale pink silk gauze, with pearls, and Alice in a softly

209

flowered silk that needed no jewels. All the world came up to shake their hands and smile and take quick, keen looks at their faces, for everyone was telling everyone that the Laceys were to have a court battle with Miss Alice—they had actually come to blows, were fighting like cats, were appealing to the Attorney-General, Chancery, the House of Lords.

The world was disappointed for the ladies looked perfectly amiable. Laura was at the peak of gratification, flashing bright smiles and green jewels and trying to forget that the jellies had not set. Marianne looked demure and at the same time inviting, and Miss Alice's welcoming smile hid the fact that her eyes were always going to the front door.

When the Prime Minister came slowly up the stairs and bent over her hand, Laura's cup was full. It was a pity dear Geoffrey looked so haggard, but this was Laura's hour and she glowed.

Alice's came almost immediately after, when Matthew Vale greeted the Laceys punctiliously, bowed with a twinkle at Marianne, and finally raised Alice's hand to his lips. She drew him a little way from the group at the head of the stairs. 'Have you discovered anything?' she asked him anxiously in a whisper.

'Only that your brother left the House early. He could easily have been home before you returned last night yourself.'

Alice's hand flew to her mouth. 'Does that mean he killed Josephus?' she asked in barely audible tones. It was like a melodrama, but so very different. The tale demanded ruins and moonlight and the squawking of malevolent crows, yet here Alice was standing in her very best dress, pressing the hands of the cream of London society.

'Stop it!' whispered Matthew Vale quite sharply, and she realized she was shaking from head to toe. 'Your brother could have killed the old man, but I doubt very much if he did.'

210

'You are saying that to spare my feelings.'

'Not at all. Listen and stop worrying. I am here to do the worrying from now on. I am late tonight because I have been consulting a surgeon—the most knowledge-able one I could find. Josephus was lying peaceably, you said, did you not, with his eyes open? Yes? I thought so. Well, in the surgeon's opinion, if he had been smothered with a pillow, there would have been signs of a struggle. Do you understand? His arms and legs would have been twisted in all directions and his eyes would most cer-tainly have been closed. The body as you described it in your letter was that of a man who had died naturally. He would have been dead when your brother reached him.'

'Thank heaven! Oh, I am so relieved.'

'Sir Geoffrey—if it was Sir Geoffrey—took the locket from his neck, but nothing more.'

Colour flooded into Alice's face and her eyes dwelt on Matthew gratefully.

'About the other matter . . .' he was beginning, when Laura started to turn towards them. 'I think we are through at last,' she said gladly. 'Geoffrey, shall we join the dancers?'

'There is one more carriage,' said Marianne, looking down the staircase. 'Why, it is Mrs Gorman! One did not expect her to come tonight.'

The dowager came up the stairs like a stately storm cloud. She was dressed in her usual widow's weeds, but had thrown a vast black silk shawl around her shoulders.

'I would not normally have left my home, Laura,' she said, panting a little because of the weight she carried, 'were it not for the need to express my great gratitude to this young lady and her capable maid. How are you, my dear? We are deeply obliged to you. The boy is the picture of my dear, dead Tobias, and Violet insists that we put a St George in his name, as she declares he owes his life to you.'

Laura would have been as well pleased if Mrs Gorman had spared herself the need to demonstrate her gratitude. For now she was surrounded by well-wishers and congratulations when Laura, in a fever of unnecessary impatience, wanted to get everybody to the dance floor. 'You must come inside,' she said to Mrs Gorman.

'No, I shall stay here and have a few words with Alice and my friends,' said Mrs Gorman, sinking on to a gilt chair that had been put there for artistic reasons. 'John said he would come for me in fifteen minutes. He is with Violet, of course.'

Laura had just cleared a path for herself when there was one last scurry of arrival at the door. 'Now who can that be?' she asked vexedly. 'It is too hard if people cannot come on time.'

Two sturdy sailors entered, followed by two stalwart blacks in bright livery. Between them, on poles, they carried a strange, high, elongated box covered with old leather and brass studs.

'Great Scott! It is a sedan chair,' said one of the gentlemen looking over the bannisters. 'I have not seen one of those since I was in short frocks.'

'Where did it come from? A museum?'

'Do look, William. A sedan! And two fellows from the Empire Circus. Is it a joke, Lady Lacey? Will they perform?'

Laura was not pleased. The unusual did not appeal to her, and her programme was being thrown awry. 'Find what is in that thing and have it sent away,' she called down to the butler. 'I cannot think why it was brought here at all. There must be some mistake.'

'Bain't a thing. Tes a she,' called up a sailor respectfully.

'What does he mean? What is it? Look inside.'

'I don't know how to open it, my lady,' said the butler, who was poking helplessly at its further side.

'You lifts the lid,' explained the sailor, doing it, 'and you pulls the front open—there!' And the inside of the sedan chair came into open view. It was lined with white quilted satin, rather musty, and in the very middle of the seat, with a very straight back and a head of beautiful snow-white hair, all dressed in black without a single relieving ornament, sat a small, strange, determined-looking old lady with a tight little nutcracker face.

She cast her eyes all round the hall and then looked upward to meet at least forty eyes, all staring down at her, some alarmed, some amused, all intrigued.

'I have come to visit my cousin, Miss Alice Lacey,' she announced in high, very precise tones.

'Great Heavens!' cried Marianne, coming forward to see what all the fuss was about. 'It is Great-Aunt Euphemie!'

Her hand flew to her bosom. She had just been about to dance with Captain Wargate, and her other hand still lay in his.

'And why, Miss, may I ask, are you not in mourning?' came up the voice with piercing clarity. 'Your grandfather is barely cold in his grave.'

'There is a ball, Aunt.'

'So I can see. But was it for balls that you came to London? You told me it was to choose bridal clothes and linen. I must look into this.' She gestured to her two strong servants from St Kitts, who came forward as one, took the old lady's arms with practised gentleness and more or less carried her up the stairs and put her down on the gilt chair from which Mrs Gorman had risen to get a better view.

The clear, high tones continued untroubled all the way up the staircase. 'Are we not to keep the fifth commandment, then?' demanded Great-Aunt Euphemie. 'Should we not honour our parents—grandparent in your case, Marianne? *Honore ton père et ta Mère, afin que tes jours soient prolongés sur la terre que l'Eternel ton Dieu te donne.* What will *le Bon Dieu* think when he looks down on all this reckless junketting?' and she stared at Laura in a way which made her quail, 'and considers the dear, dead body of the departed—for-

213

gotten, while his soul is yet on its way to heaven? Eh, Marianne? What do you mean by it, Miss?'

'Put this over you,' came a helpful contralto whisper, and Marianne found herself draped in Mrs Gorman's voluminous black shawl. She had no time for thanks before Great-Aunt Euphemie was off again.

'Who is that young man?' she enquired, gazing piercingly at Captain Wargate. He bowed with a flourish, and rolled out his name and regiment, finishing with an engaging smile. 'Very much at your service, ma'am,' he said.

'Why were you holding my great-niece's hand? Marianne, is he a relative of ours? I do not recollect the name.'

'No, Tante Euphemie.'

'And does he know who you are to be? My niece, Captain Wargate,' she informed him severely, 'is the affianced bride of James Hervey de la Brète Hammond, the son of Sir Frederick Hammond of River Fields and High Harbour Plantations on St Kitts and various properties in Martinique. On the French side, the family is noble.'

'Marianne,' breathed Alice. 'Why did you not tell me? You should not—we ought not to have—I should never have let you go into society without this being known.'

Marianne cast her eyes down, then gave a small toss of her head and finally broke into a smile. 'That is the very reason why I could not tell you, Alice,' she said. 'Surely you can see?'

'Alice!' repeated the old woman. 'Is that my cousin? Dear Amelie's child? You may come and kiss me. Why! You look just like she did when she .was very young.'

'Good evening, Miss St George.'

'You may call me Aunt. And I have quite forgiven your poor mother. She should not have married against her father's consent, but now we will let it pass.'

'Alice's mother was not married,' said Laura in

mounting frustration at the way her ball was going to pieces.

'Who are you?' demanded Great-Aunt Euphemie, her sharp dark eyes raking Laura from head to toe.

'My name is Lacey—Lady Lacey. This is my house, and I think you should have given us some warning of your arrival. We are in the middle of entertaining our guests and the Prime Minister is here, and if all Alice's relations are to pour in unasked . . .'

'Alice will welcome her aunt to her own house, will you not, child?'

'Aunt Euphemie, I . . .'

'This is not Alice's house.'

'And tell that vulgar brawling woman to hold her tongue. Where is your abominable half-brother? Where is the man who dares to deface the fair name of one who springs from the St George's? Are you the man?' she enquired of John Gorman, who was coming up the stairs to find his mother. 'Stand out, sir, so that I can see you clear. *Saligaud! Canaille!*'

John Gorman blenched. 'I do not believe we have met, ma'am,' he said uneasily.

'My husband is here!' cried Laura Lacey. 'Geoffrey, come forward. Why do you not seize this—this intruder and turn her out of the house. Oh! I have never been so insulted!'

'Young man,' said Great-Aunt Euphemie, 'you have brought down doom upon your own head, for is it not written, *ceux qui labourent l'iniquité et qui sèment l'outrage, les moissonnent?* You have wrought destruction on an innocent child. You have persecuted the orphan and shorn the lamb. *Ne vous abusez point; on ne se joue point de Dieu!*'

'Has there been an accident?' enquired the Prime Minister, looking over the heads to see why everyone had left the dance floor.

'*Il a détroné les puissants,*' continued Great-Aunt Euphemie, '*et il a élevé les petits.*'

215

'Why do you let her go on like this? Geoffrey, make her stop. This is a ball, not a—a—a French cathedral!' Laura was losing control of herself.

'He shall know,' said Great-Aunt Euphemie, opening an ancient reticule and producing a large document heavily embossed with seals. 'I have here a copy of an entry from the records of the chapel of St Thomas on the Island of Nevis, sworn as correct by three Notaries Public of Nevis and a Commissioner of Oaths from St Kitts, countersigned by the Government Attorney of the Island and endorsed by Sir Berkely Hawke, Her Majesty's Governor-General of the Leeward Islands.' She paused for breath, and her eyes swept the surrounding faces. 'Witnesseth the sacrament of marriage between Walter Percy Lacey of Wiltshire, England, to Amelie Lestrange of Nevis.'

'No!' cried Laura Lacey faintly.

'On this day of grace, the fourteenth of July, 1828,' concluded Great-Aunt Euphemie.

A shocked silence fell on the ring of observers. All eyes swung to Geoffrey Lacey. Now how could he justify the treatment he had meted out to his half-sister?

But it was Alice who made an objection. '1828!' she cried. 'But that is impossible.' A strong hand on her shoulder told her that Matthew Vale was giving her his support.

'I will pardon your lack of politeness, Alice,' said the elder Miss St George, 'and put it down to the excitement.'

'But Sir Walter could not have married Tante Amelie on that date,' said Marianne. 'He was on Nevis, yes, but he came straight home and married another lady.'

'May God have mercy on his soul,' said Great-Aunt Euphemie, 'for he was a wicked man.'

'Do you mean,' asked Alice, 'that my father married Geoffrey's mother when he was already married to my mother? He contracted a second marriage whilst his first wife was alive and well?'

'Lacey, I think you should take steps to silence that old lady,' John Gorman said to the white-faced Geoffrey. 'She is casting very grave suspicions on your birth.'

But it was Alice who took up the cudgels yet again. 'Dear Aunt Euphemie,' she said very seriously, 'I cannot answer for my father's moral condition, but I know that my dearest mother would never live with a man who committed bigamy. She would know that he had broken the sacrament.'

'No she wouldn't' boomed out a voice unexpectedly.

'What do you mean, Mrs Gorman?'

'If Amelie were married herself by a Catholic priest, she would not consider Daisy Stebbings' marriage to her husband legal or binding. Marriages in the English church do not count with us at all.'

'Geoffrey!' cried Laura. 'Make them stop! Say it is not true. Make that nasty old woman go away.' But one look at her husband's bowed shoulders told her to expect no help from him. 'What does it mean?' asked Laura frantically turning from face to face. Quicker wits than hers had worked out that the so-called Laceys had no entitlement to the good things they had been enjoying since Sir Walter's death. Alice's fortune should never have been taken from her—yes, Laura could comprehend that. But shocked faces, quick murmerings and the sudden dropping of lids when she sought sympathetic eyes among her friends told her that the case was much worse than that.

'I don't understand,' said Laura helplessly.

'It seems your husband's parents were not married at law, my dear,' said Mrs Gorman, not unkindly. 'No doubt it will be sorted out by the attorneys, but I should say everything belongs to Alice now—lock, stock and barrel.'

'No!' Laura's cry of anguish would have melted stone. 'Alice,' she turned on her sister-in-law. 'I don't understand what it all means, but you were always kind. Dear Alice. Of course you get back all the Lacey things, that

217

is proper—here, take the emeralds. But it doesn't mean that all Geoffrey's things belong to you too, does it? Alice, say something . . . I can't bear it . . . oh!'

'I should not wish to profit by any harm my father did to an unfortunate woman,' Alice said very slowly, and the pressure on her shoulder remained steady.

Geoffrey's head jerked up. 'I am not accepting charity from you, Alice,' he snarled.

'Now come, come, Lacey, you must take it like a man,' said John Gorman, putting his arm around his friend. 'We will get you to your room.'

'His name is not Lacey,' said the high voice of Great-Aunt Euphemie. 'There is only one Lacey and that is my niece.'

'So there is. Well, never mind. Come on, old fellow. Come on—er—Stebbings.'

'Stebbings!' said Laura and fell into a deep swoon.

'And what do you mean, young man, by clasping my niece in that unlicensed way?' demanded the indefatigable Great-Aunt Euphemie. 'I had heard that the moral tone of London was much improved, but this is beyond belief. As it is said in Deuteronomy, young man, *prends garde à toi, que tu n'aies dans ton coeur quelque méchante intention.* Who are you? Where do you come from? What is your estate?'

'I am the man who is to marry Miss Alice Lacey,' said Matthew Vale, not in the least disconcerted. He raised the old lady's hand to his lips. 'I trust we shall meet to-morrow and I am sure that I shall enjoy your company, but for the moment I am taking Alice for a drive in the park.'

'You are not, sir. It would be most improper.'

'But I am. She has had more than enough to bear for one evening and she needs a little quiet to recover. I shall take great care of her.'

'Oh Matthew, I cannot leave. Who will help Laura?'

'Somebody else. Come, my love.'

'But there is no-one to look after the guests. The servants . . .'

'They will do very well by themselves.'

'I have no shawl,' cried Alice, following the implacable pull of his arm.

'Here, take this,' said Marianne, running down the staircase behind them. 'I do not want black any more tonight. It will be nothing else tomorrow.'

'Marianne,' whispered Alice rapidly, turning her head over her shoulder as she was propelled through the front door, 'That James Hervey, the man you are to marry, do you care for him?'

'But of course,' said Marianne, opening her eyes very wide. 'My heart goes with my hand. What would you expect?'

'I am so glad,' said Alice, and gave herself up to the pure pleasure of being with Mr Vale.